BOOKS BY BETH PRENTICE

The Westport Mysteries

Lizzie

A Sinister Sign ~ The Prequel

Dangerous Deeds

Give Murder A Hand

Deathly Desire

The Christmas Gift – A Mini Lizzie Mystery

Molly

Wicked Little Lies

Chloe

Killer Unleashed

Deadly Tails

Alexandra

Invitation to Murder

Gracie

The Ivory Veil – a novella

The Aloha Lagoon Samantha Reynolds Mysteries

Deadly Wipeout

Lethal Tide

Fatal Break

Tidal Wave

The Dandelion Ponds Mysteries

In High Spirits

The Hollyday Spirit - novella

That's the Spirit

The Dun Roamin' Romantic Mysteries

Tilly ~ Before Dun Roamin'

Matilda's Wish

THAT'S THE SPIRIT

THE DANDELION PONDS MYSTERIES
BOOK THREE

BETH PRENTICE

PROLOGUE

The dead of night closed in as old, dark iron gates towered above me, a thick metal chain hanging from the large skull and cross bones welded to the rails, poison ivy winding its way around the lock. Flames leaped from torches high above the gates, and the black arch held a sign—*The Lethal Garden*.

Voices from deep within the courtyard floated to me on the breeze—voices that were not friendly.

I needed to hear what they were saying, innately knowing their words could save my life.

Taking a step closer to the gates I bit my lip wondering how to get inside when I noticed the padlock hung loose, unlocked by those who'd entered before me.

Slowly reaching out, I pushed open the gate, willing it to be silent. I was in someone's dream, and I wasn't meant to be there. Whose dream it was, I had yet to learn.

Moving quickly toward the voices, I hid in the shadows of the laburnum trees, stepping carefully around the castor oil plant knowing its toxin was deadly. Large yellow flowers of angel's trumpet hung waiting to be picked by someone lured by its noxious beauty. Midnight bluebells of wolf's bane swayed in the breeze, just waiting to kill. Deadly nightshade trailed across the dirt, and I held my breath as I passed the noxious, cyanogenic fumes of the laurel.

Every dazzling plant in this lovingly tended garden had the ability to kill, to destroy lives with a simple touch. I knew how deadly they were, yet their beauty was bewitching, enticing me to pick their flowers, but I had to resist their intoxicating perfume and stay focused. I crossed my arms over my chest and pulled my gaze away breaking the spell they cast.

The warning came from across the garden. "We must wait for the precise moment." The woman's long black dress and cloak told me she was from another time. "Once the lunar eclipse has passed, it must be the first moonlight that falls on the leaves. That's what makes it so powerful." She held a potted plant, the silver foliage almost sparkling under the moonlight.

"Valeria, be careful. It's far more dangerous than you know."

"Don't worry, my sister. I know what I'm doing. If I get this right, then I will become the first night demon. With that power I can control everyone." She cackled.

"But what about me?"

"You will be the second, and together we will rule them all."

1

I snapped my eyes open and glanced around the room, grounding myself. Spending time in other people's dreams left me feeling strange and out of sorts, but this one in particular left me shaken. I had no idea why I was so scared as I usually took comfort from my dreams.

"Daisy, were you daydreaming again?"

I blinked against the glare of the overhead hospital lighting and spun to the man sitting alongside my hospital bed, inhaling sharply as his smoke-grey eyes looked into my soul. He had a perfect set of dimples, sexy five o'clock shadow, and was a dangerous mix of vulnerability and masculinity.

"Yes, and it wasn't fun." I placed my hand over my heart and willed the fear to flee as visions of the garden caused a weight to sit in my soul. "When am I ever going to slip into someone's dream while they're chatting with Chris Hemsworth?" I joked, not wanting to relive the dream by replaying it out loud.

"Only chatting with him?" Charlie raised a quizzical eyebrow. We'd only met a short time ago, but he already knew me so well.

"Okay, maybe he'd be shirtless at the time." I chuckled as Charlie's warmth pushed the cold away. "Now would you stop staring at me like that." I hated people staring at me. It made me hyperaware of the freckles scattered across my nose, my sallow skin, and my chapped lips. And the way the sheet was tucked tight against my body did nothing to enhance my bust, even though spending weeks in a coma had definitely helped narrow my waistline. I guess there really was an upside to everything.

Charlie's smile reached megawatt status as he looked away from the me lying in the bed then back at the me he was conversing with.

"No! Not me," I explained jabbing a thumb at my chest. "Me." I turned and pointed at my physical body lying on the hospital bed.

Shortly before Christmas a failed attempt had been made on my life, leaving me in a coma, stuck somewhere between life and death. My little Chihuahua, Alfie, had called to me, and my spirit had woken up in a strange man's bedroom. The man, aka Charlie, was one of two people who could see me, and he happened to be a blessing—despite the fact that at the moment he was studying my unconscious body and making me feel extremely uncomfortable.

"But you're so cute." Charlie beamed, the crinkles around his eyes deepening.

"Really? I think I look terrible. I mean, check out my greasy hair." My ash blonde curls were tucked behind my ears. My long eyelashes curled without the help of a mascara wand, and my features were relaxed. Admittedly, I appeared peaceful, but as my emotions were felt with my soul I knew the truth of what was really going on inside.

Charlie chuckled, and a delicious thrill danced down my spine.

"Just adds to your charm." He wriggled his eyebrows as he pointedly gazed at my spirited face.

"What does my spirit look like to you?" I asked, attempting to fiddle with a loose thread hanging from the hem of my

Christmas pajamas and making a silent promise to myself if I woke up, I'd always go to bed looking my best. It appeared my mother had been right, and you just never knew when you were going to get hit by a bus. Or in my case, have someone attempt to murder you.

"What do you mean?"

"Well, I look down at my hands and I see them, but when I try to touch them it's like grabbing fog. They're not really there." I wiggled my spirit fingers to demonstrate.

Charlie shook his head. "You look whole to me, only your color is a little less vibrant than a full-bodied person."

"Is that how you see the other spirits who usually hang around with us?" I asked, referring to my new friends Frank and Elsie.

"No. They're transparent."

Well, that was interesting. "Do you think that means I have a chance of rejoining the living anytime soon?" Hanging around as a spirit had its advantages, but I couldn't wait to be reunited with my body. I missed the little things like the wind on my face and the scent of freshly cut flowers.

"You are living."

"Okay," I responded, rolling my eyes. "Do you think I have any chance of rejoining the *conscious* anytime soon." I grinned.

Charlie nodded. "I think so. Your color gets more vibrant every single day."

My shoulders relaxed as a warm feeling started around my heart, and the monitor attached to my sleeping body gave an erratic little beep. Charlie had that effect on me. Apart from the fact he was extremely good-looking and had more muscles than I'd ever seen, he was fun, caring, and had the ability to make my pulse race just a little bit faster.

"You must be getting closer," he continued, gently touching the back of my sleeping hand. "The reactions your spirit experiences are affecting your body more and more."

The monitor went berserk. It appeared my unconscious self had an even bigger reaction to Charlie.

Urgh! As technically I was still engaged to another man, this was a really bad thing.

"I wish I could write," I mused.

"Why?"

"My mental list of things to do when I wake up is getting too long for me to remember everything. I need to have something in writing."

"I'm good at those." Charlie pulled his phone from the back pocket of his jeans and his long fingers started to tap on the screen. "All right. I've titled it 'Things for Daisy to Do.' Tell me everything."

"You may regret this." I laughed, tapping my fluffy sock against the cushion of air beneath my feet. "Okay, job number one is to buy some new pajamas."

"What's wrong with the ones you're wearing? I think they're kind of sexy."

Oh boy.

"You're a weird man, Charlie O'Sullivan."

He shrugged. "I've been called worse. Now what's number two on the list?"

I was about to say, *Call my fiancé and tell him the engagement is over*, but that would raise too many questions from Charlie, questions I just wasn't ready to answer. Plus, that was a conversation I should first have with Logan.

"Job number two is to reopen my flower shop. It's sad seeing the doors closed this time of year."

I stared absently at the small tree sitting on the table next to my bed, unsure whether I was sad it would soon be removed or happy a new year was about to start. The week between Christmas and New Year's Day was always a busy time for a florist. In past years I would have already been pulling down some of the Christmas decorations and swapping them out for much more celebratory bouquets. The Christmas wreaths would be changed to party ribbons, banners would be strung behind the counter, and champagne baskets would become my biggest order. I sighed, missing my little shop more and more with each passing day.

The steady beep of the monitors attached to my body were the soundtrack of the sterile-looking room, the bouquet of yellow gerberas on my bedside table a much-needed splash of color. The fluorescent lighting flooded the space, shining against the plastic oxygen tube tucked under my nose and highlighting the feeding tube taped around my rosebud lips. I slept like I hadn't a care in the world. If only my soul felt that much peace.

"When am I going to wake up?"

"When you're ready."

"I am ready!"

"Then something must be stopping you. Can you think what that could be?"

My sigh came from deep within. "No. I spend every single second of the night thinking about it, and so far I have nothing." It appeared sleeping wasn't something a spirit stuck between two worlds was able to do, which was a real buzzkill as dreams were my superpower—quite literally. But I'd only recently learned I was a night demon.

Now, I know that sounds terrible, and it kind of is, as night demons visit people in their dreams and often make them do horrible things. But I only use my newfound powers for good, and I never deliberately pop in to spy on anyone's dreams. Okay, I may have popped into Charlie's dream once, but when I saw him kissing his guardian angel, Anastasia, I hurriedly removed myself and vowed to never do that again...unless it helped me get to the bottom of all the strange events happening in town lately. Then I'd maybe do it again. But only maybe.

My small hometown of Dandelion Ponds wasn't a big place. Its population was around seven thousand. We had two churches, one hospital, and one shopping center. Plus, it was headquarters for a coven of night demons who had previously tried to recruit me, but my father had protected me right up until the day he died. Then his power had been passed to me along with his small fortune. Shame he'd never thought to tell me all of this while he'd had a chance. It definitely would have made my life a lot easier.

"Have you tried putting yourself back together lately?" Charlie asked, perching himself on the edge of my bed.

"Not for a day or so."

"Try now." He patted the mattress.

"It's a waste of time." I pouted

"Come on. It can't hurt, and you just never know what's going to happen. Plus, there's something I want to try." He flashed a lobsided grin, and my heart melted. It appeared I'd lost complete control of my actions whenever Charlie was involved. "Do you trust me?" He gazed into my soul, and my monitors spiked.

"Completely." I couldn't hide my grin as I moved alongside my sleeping self before hopping up and lying directly on top of my body, aligning myself perfectly. I closed my eyes and willed my soul to reunite with my living cells. Lately the reactions of my physical body were felt by my soul, which had to mean I was getting closer to being whole again, right?

Charlie stirred alongside me, and I heard the sheets rustle. Seconds later a warm whisper of breath danced across my cheek and a jolt of electricity zinged down my spine. My eyes shot open as Charlie placed a delicate kiss on my cheek, his own eyes closed, a smile playing in their corners.

I sighed as our souls connected. It was a common reaction I had to him, and one I never wanted to take for granted. Today however, the pull was stronger.

"Do that again," I pleaded quietly.

His eyelids blinked open. "Did you feel something?"

Did I ever. "Your breath...on my cheek," I explained, lifting my hand to my face, my thoughts jumbled. "I've never felt that before."

He swallowed hard. "Want to try it again?"

Words failed me, so I nodded my consent.

"Close your eyes," he whispered, placing a hand on either side of my body as he leaned in close. I stifled my blissful sigh and did as asked before heat blasted my lips. His kiss was soft and delicate, and desire flashed through every cell I owned as my sleeping self stirred.

"It's working," he whispered, his voice croaky. His smile was dreamy as his eyes lingered on my lips, and the background monitors played a symphony.

I lifted my spirited hand and wiggled my fingers. "I think my sleeping body is just having a reaction to you."

"Then we should do it again. Your body's responding. That's a good sign."

I was about to add that my soul was responding too as my spirit had ached with the need for his touch, but the desire was quashed as the door to my room flung open, and both Charlie and I looked toward the angry gasp travelling across the room.

Logan Cutter stood tall, his hands jammed into the pockets of his open jacket, his designer stubble highlighting the tight line of his mouth. His dark jeans hugged his backside and his t-shirt looked like it was sprayed onto his toned torso.

"Get away from my fiancée," he growled, his emerald-green eyes locked onto Charlie, his teeth bared into a scowl.

Uh-oh.

The rubber soles of his sneakers squeaked against the vinyl floor as his long legs strode across the room.

Charlie groaned as a heaviness settled into his soul. I knew. I could feel it.

He pushed off the bed and moved away from me, his own jaw set hard as he faced up to Logan. "Hello to you, too." He scowled, his dislike for Logan plastered in his sneer.

I sat up straight, my eyes wide, worried as to how this would play out.

"How many times do I have to tell you to stay away from Daisy?" Logan jabbed a finger into Charlie's chest, his creased brow disappearing into the dark widow's peak at the center of his forehead.

Charlie ground his teeth as his jaw clenched. "What do you care?"

"Are you serious?" Logan demanded, moving in dangerously close and pulling himself up to his full height.

"From what I can tell, you barely seem to care about Daisy. You rarely visit her and only seem interested in yourself."

"For your information, I visit her every day." Logan's voice cracked on the last words, and he averted his gaze.

As I had no idea what happened to my sleeping body when my spirit wasn't around, I had no way to know if he was telling the truth.

"Huh, well it's convenient you're never there when she needs you," Charlie finished.

Logan swallowed hard as I gasped.

"Charlie!" I scolded. "That's not fair." Innocent until proven guilty, right?

His gaze momentarily flicked to me.

"Yeah, but it's convenient *you* are!" Logan spat, his shoulders rigid, completely unaware of my presence.

"What do you mean by that?"

"For a guy who says he never knew Daisy before she fell into a coma, you sure hang around her a lot. What are you? Some kind of pervert?"

Charlie dismissed Logan with a glance. "You don't deserve her," he said under his breath.

"Daisy would disagree."

"I don't think so." Charlie shook his head and took a step closer to me.

Logan opened his mouth to respond, but the hospital door swung open once again—only this time Charlie's mother, Dorothy, stuck her head around the corner.

"Yoo-hoo!" She beamed as she stepped into the room. Remnants of snow balanced on the lengths of her fire engine red locks which poked from beneath a crocheted hat. Her tie-dyed scarf flapped open over her red cable-knit jumper, and her long gypsy skirt swirled around her yellow polka dot rubber boots. Her oversized tote bag seemed to wiggle with a life of its own.

She didn't need her psychic abilities to gauge the energy in the room, and her gaze flipped between the two men.

"Well, well, well. Logan Cutter. How are you?" she asked, stepping between them. Her shoulders tensed, and I wasn't sure whether she was protecting Charlie from Logan or vice versa. Either way, she was a mother in protection mode.

Logan had enough sense or manners to take a step backward and reassess his attitude. Town gossip had Dorothy pegged as a witch, and even though Logan had told me he didn't believe in such things, he tended to err on the side of caution.

"Mrs. O'Leary." He nodded in lieu of hello.

"So, what's going on here?" she asked, placing her bag on the floor. Instantly it shimmied, and a small yap sounded from within. Charlie leaned down, pulled back the zipper, and the little black nose of my Chihuahua, Alfie, poked out.

"Mom!" Charlie reprimanded. "You can't bring a dog in here. The hospital has rules against it."

"Tsk," she replied, waving her hand dismissively. "He wanted to see Daisy, and I know she wants to see him. Maybe he's just what she needs to wake up. It seems she doesn't want to wake for either of you."

Ready to argue, Logan's mouth dropped open, but as Dorothy crossed her arms over her chest and raised her eyebrows, he hurriedly snapped his lips together.

At least it had diffused the tension between the men. If only temporarily.

"Alfie," I cried as he bounded toward me. Despite the fact I couldn't touch him, I knelt in front of him and inhaled his aura. He immediately spun in circles, his eyes bright, his tongue flapping to the side. All my tension dissolved.

Dorothy winked at me then moved to Alfie and lifted him onto the bed. As he licked the chin of my sleeping body, a warm feeling started to grow around my heart.

"Why haven't we tried this before?" I muttered, wondering if this was exactly what I needed.

"There's something special about this dog," she explained.

"We always did have a unique connection."

Dorothy nodded, the bobble on the end of her hat wobbling as she moved. "He's your familiar."

"My what?"

"Familiar. It's an animal with the capability of heightening your abilities."

"Oh, I'm not sure about that, but I do feel calmer when he's around."

"He called you to Charlie, didn't he?"

"Who's she talking to?" Logan demanded, his voice loud and echoing in the room.

To be fair, Logan couldn't see my spirit, and it would look like Dorothy was talking to herself.

"She's chatting to Daisy." Charlie threw him a glare.

"Does she think Daisy can respond, does she?" Sarcasm laced Logan's words.

"She can. You just can't hear her."

Logan's eyes widened. "Are you kidding me? Daisy is in a coma. I know they say people in comas can hear, but they can't respond."

"She's talking to Daisy's spirit."

Logan's jaw dropped.

"Daisy's spirit is sitting right in front of her," Charlie continued, pointing directly at me.

"Really?" I cautioned, before standing. "I don't think it's a good idea, Charlie. Logan isn't ready to know you can see my spirit."

"I don't care what Logan's ready for. It's the truth," Charlie replied, exasperated.

Logan's jaw tensed.

"I don't care about you either," he snarled. "The only thing I care about is getting you to stay away from Daisy."

"Logan," Dorothy interjected, "if having Charlie close helps Daisy, then that's a good thing."

Logan's eyes bulged as he stammered to respond. "Good… good thing? He's a psycho! I walked in here to find him kissing a woman in a coma!"

Dorothy's gaze flipped to Charlie as she struggled to hide her smirk.

"You kissed her?" she asked.

Color raced up Charlie's neck only stopping as it reached his ears.

"If Daisy were awake, she'd have you arrested," Logan continued, ignoring the glee in Dorothy's eyes. "In fact, maybe I should do just that." A vein in his neck pulsed as he jammed his fist into his jeans pocket and retrieved his phone.

Charlie's jaw clenched. "If Daisy were awake, I know which one of us she'd be reporting to the police."

"I want you both out of here," Logan yelled. "I'm calling security."

"Go for it!" Charlie retaliated. "They won't do your bidding. You don't have Daisy's old BFF, Lilli, here to help you with her powers anymore."

I gulped as the sound of her name caused painful memories to stir. Lilli, too, was a night demon. We'd had a bond closer than I had with my sister, but recently I'd learned exactly what she was prepared to do with her powers. And believe me, it was never good.

"Leave her out of this!" Logan spat.

"Why? It's all true."

"Lilli never helped me like that."

"As if I'd believe that," Charlie replied disdainfully.

Logan looked wrong-footed as he stepped backwards, rubbing his face. A bead of sweat broke out on his forehead, and his breathing came deep and fast.

"Charlie, stop," I cried, my emotions tangled. "He feels guilty enough about what happened. You don't need to reinforce it."

Charlie moved his eyes to meet mine. "You're defending him?"

"No! It's just that this isn't achieving anything."

"Who are you talking to?" Logan yelled.

"Daisy!" Charlie and Dorothy both yelled.

"He can't see me," I screamed throwing my hands in the air.

"He can't feel you either," Charlie snapped, taking a step closer to my sleeping body. As his hand touched mine, his voice softened. "Not like I can. And not like you can feel me."

Gently lifting my hand to his lips, he kissed my fingertips. My insides melted, and my heart rate monitor went berserk.

Logan moved beside me, shoved Charlie aside and took my hand in his own. Copying Charlie, he kissed my palm, but much to his dismay, my monitor only slowed back to its steady rhythm.

His eyes hardened as his lips trembled. Squeezing my hand tight, he leaned down and kissed me firmly on the lips.

I moved to stand alongside him, but my heart ached, and I knew what I had once felt for him was no longer there. I still loved him, but not in the same way I was falling for Charlie.

Maybe Dorothy was right when she'd said you only ever have one soul mate.

Silence descended on us all as Logan gulped, his jaw tense. Blinking back tears, he slowly lowered my hand to the sheets.

"It'll be different when she wakes up. She won't be under

any spells you have over her." He pointed his accusation to Dorothy. His fingers flexed as he spun to face Charlie. "Until then I suggest you get out of here and stay away from her. Or else."

"Or else what?"

Logan's voice was low and menacing as he jabbed Charlie in the chest. "Or else I'll kill you."

Charlie released a bark of laughter and swatted the hand away. "Good luck trying."

Logan reddened before pulling his shoulder back and clenching his fist. As he swung toward Charlie, Charlie ducked, and Logan stumbled from his own force.

I squealed, Alfie yapped, and Dorothy stomped her foot as she forced her hands on her hips.

"Boys!" she yelled. Only neither of them listened.

Logan hurriedly regained his balance then lunged at Charlie, knocking them both to the floor. Dorothy rolled her eyes before reaching into her bag and retrieving a small brown bottle. Unscrewing the lid filled the room with the scent of bergamot and lavender.

"Blessed be, breathe calm into thee, and allow the scent to soothe." She chanted as she sprinkled the potion over the men.

It took a moment, but Logan's eyes glazed over, and Charlie pushed him off.

"Hurry and get up," Dorothy demanded. "The potion only lasts a moment. He'll be back to his angry self in a second."

"What did you do that for?" Charlie demanded, rubbing his nose as he got to his feet. "I'm perfectly capable of controlling Logan."

"Yeah, it looked that way," she snapped, smacking her lips into a tight line.

"Charlie, please," I begged. "Calm down."

"I'm not the one who started it," he reminded me.

"I know. But Logan's just…lost."

Charlie held my gaze as his thoughts flashed through his eyes. Anger dissolved into confusion and finally settled on hurt.

His jaw tensed as his fists balled, and he lowered his gaze to the floor as he took some slow breaths. "I'm going home. It seems I'm not wanted here."

"Don't be like that," I pleaded. "I just need to wake up and explain everything to Logan and then life can...move on."

Charlie nodded as he grabbed his jacket from chair and then stomped from the room.

Moments later Logan shook himself off and stood, his gaze unfocused. He glared at Dorothy before stumbling after Charlie and almost knocking over the nurse in blue scrubs who had poked her head around the door.

"Is everything okay in here?" she asked, glaring at Logan before moving toward my monitors and pressing a few buttons.

"Sorry, Amanda. Charlie and Logan just didn't see eye to eye on something," Dorothy explained.

"So, I heard." She grimaced. "After everything Daisy has been through, Logan's pretty protective of her." Amanda had been one of my nurses since my arrival at the Dandelion Ponds Regional Hospital and had met most of my family and friends who regularly visited me. Through her attentiveness she'd often been privy to some of their most private feelings.

"Yeah, the testosterone was pumping." Dorothy grinned good naturedly. "But Charlie only has her best interest at heart."

Amanda nodded. "Lucky girl having two men fighting over her. Anyway, Daisy seems unperturbed, so I'll leave you to sit with her for a while."

Once the door had closed behind her, I turned to Dorothy.

"Should we be worried about them?" I asked.

"Nah. As soon as Logan gets outside the weather will sober him up, and all effects of the potion will wear off."

"Why didn't it have the same effect on Charlie?"

"Years of living with me…he's built-up immunity to some of my more frequently used spells." She grinned.

Alfie had remained by my side throughout the entire showdown, so I sat beside him and soaked up his energy. Within moments I felt better.

"So," started Dorothy, "Charlie kissed you."

As much as I wanted to, I couldn't hide my grin. "Ahuh."

"And?"

"And what?"

"What happened?" Dorothy pulled the chair alongside my bed and perched on the edge of it.

I took a moment to relive the feeling in my mind before filling Dorothy in with the details.

"He's your soul mate, Daisy. He holds the key to you waking up. I just know it."

"If that's true, why am I still asleep? I want to be with him. And I want to tell Logan the truth. It's not his fault I fell for another man while I slept. And before you say anything I know he hasn't been completely honest with me, and I do feel betrayed by him. But he deserves an explanation about what's happening between me and Charlie. Otherwise, I'm no better than he is."

"Tell me about him. What made you think you were once in love with him? What made you say yes to his marriage proposal?"

Dorothy sat back in the chair readying herself for a story. Alfie lay down alongside my body, and I absently stroked his back.

"Well…" I started. Only I didn't get to finish as the sound of sirens screaming through the afternoon broke through my memories.

Dorothy jumped up and rushed to the window, me hot on her heels.

"What on earth is going on out there?" I asked as a loud *pop* echoed over my shoulder.

"Dorothy." Dulcet tones startled me, and I spun to see a Chanel-clad glamazon staring at us both.

"Oh my goodness, Anastasia," I called, my heart racing, "what are you doing here?" Ana was Charlie's guardian angel, but after a recent falling out they'd had over her ex-boyfriend she'd been absent for a short while. I wondered if her reappearance meant he'd moved her into the forgiven file.

Ana ignored me; her gaze locked onto Dorothy.

"What's wrong?" Dorothy asked, standing to meet her.

"Charlie needs your help."

Dorothy's eyes widened. "Is he hurt?"

"No. Physically Charlie's fine. It's Logan."

"What about him?" I asked, the hair on the back of my neck rising.

Ana moved her gaze to me, and she gulped. "I'm sorry, Daisy, but Logan's dead."

2

A light dusting of snow gathered on Logan's body as he lay faceup on the footpath, red liquid pooling from the wound to his neck. His hand was wet with his blood as if he'd tried to save his own life as he'd stumbled along the path.

A small crowd had gathered as paramedics moved rapidly around Logan, attaching various leads to his pale skin. Their expressions told the story.

Charlie stood back from the crowd, leaning against the wall separating the parking lot from the hospital, his eyes wide. Blood smeared the front of his jacket. Dorothy rushed toward him.

"Mom! I'm glad you're here." His lips trembled as he grabbed her hand.

"Are you hurt?" Her voice wobbled on her last word as she scanned his clothing.

He slowly shook his head, his eyes locking onto Logan.

Ignoring them, I rushed to Logan's side, pushing passed the uniformed medic.

"We need to get these people out of here." The paramedic looked up at his colleague. "We've gathered quite a crowd."

"The police are here now," replied his sidekick, his breath

19

hanging in a vapor of cold air. "They'll clear the scene pretty quickly."

Red and blue lights flashed against the snow drifts and glittered in the tinsel still tied to the nearby lamp posts. Officer Trent Shelby pushed open the door to his patrol car and trudged his way toward us ducking under the Season's Greetings banner, melted snow flicking up the pant leg of his police uniform. His jacket was open at the front, which had more to do with the fact the zipper no longer met in the middle than the air temperature, and his scowl betrayed his dislike for finding dead bodies. A pretty female officer scurried after him, her skin pale as she perused the scene.

I'd never met her before, and I figured she was the replacement officer the town had been waiting for.

Shelby stopped in his tracks when he saw Charlie, and his mouth dropped open.

"I found him that way," Charlie hurriedly called.

Shelby's lips snapped shut as his jaw clenched, momentarily holding Charlie's gaze. He then ordered the female officer to get the crowd back before he moved to the paramedics. As they got lost in conversation, I stared down at the ashen face of my fiancé, and my heart cracked. I no longer wanted to marry him, but that didn't mean I didn't still love him.

"Can you save him?" I pleaded to the paramedic who knelt beside him. His gloved hand also glowed with Logan's blood, but other than that he did nothing but sit back on his heels with a sigh.

"Why aren't they trying to help him?" I cried, wringing my hands together. My legs felt weak, and my vision tunneled as the weight in my chest became unbearable.

"Daisy," Dorothy called, her voice almost lost to the crowd. "Daisy, it's too late. He's gone."

"But they can bring him back! I've seen them do it on

television." I placed my hands on the paramedic's shoulders and closed my eyes. "Help him!"

I tried to push all the noise aside and concentrate, wanting to invade his consciousness, but only walls blocked me.

Snapping my eyes open, I took a large step backwards before rushing to Dorothy. I gave a futile attempt to grab her arm. "Dorothy, tell them to help him," I gushed.

"They did try." Ana cut in, moving alongside Charlie and standing guard. "There's nothing they can do."

Charlie glanced to me, confusion clouding his eyes.

"What happened?" Dorothy asked him.

"I have no idea. I was heading to my car, and when I rounded the corner to the parking lot, I saw him lying on the ground. I rushed to see if I could help him, but he wasn't breathing. So, I called the paramedics."

"Why didn't they help him?" I pleaded as tears filled behind my lashes.

"They tried, Daisy. They tried, but it was too late."

Placing my head in my hands, I tried to slow the panic, quiet the clanging in my ears, and process what they were saying.

How could Logan be dead? How? I'd only been standing in front of him minutes ago.

"Please stand back!" The young female officer called to the crowd.

I snapped my head up, looking from her to Shelby. "Why are the police here?" I demanded. "Do they come to all accidents?"

"Daisy, this was no accident. Logan's exterior jugular vein was sliced," Ana explained. "He bled out before anyone could stop it.'

"What?" I gasped.

"Someone walked up behind him and attacked him."

"And you know this how?" Dorothy asked her.

Ana's gazed flicked to Charlie.

"Because I asked her to stay close to him," Charlie explained. "I wanted to know what he was up to."

"You had Logan followed?" My mouth dropped open as I gaped at him.

"Only to check that he was above board and was doing the right thing by you."

"So, who did that to him?" I pressed, my tone rising with every syllable.

Ana shrugged. "I don't know."

"But you were following him! You should have seen who it was."

"I realize that! But I didn't see who they were. All I know is they were wearing a long black coat over what looked like hospital scrubs. A cap and glasses covered their face."

"You didn't follow them when they left?"

"No."

"Why?"

"Because…"—she glanced at Charlie—"because I knew Charlie wasn't far behind, and I was worried about him. I rushed to him instead. And before you say anything else, he will always be my highest priority regardless of what he's asked me to do." She placed a hand on her hip and hit me with a glare. In a previous life Ana and Charlie had been a couple. She had recently told me her purpose had never been in life. It was in death, to protect Charlie any way she could.

"Charlie O'Sullivan," Officer Shelby called, stepping purposefully toward us. "Please tell me why yet again I have found you at my crime scene."

"Unlucky I guess." Charlie sighed resignedly.

Shelby and Charlie didn't have the greatest relationship, but of late they'd begun to see eye to eye.

Shelby released an audible breath as he flipped a page in his notebook.

"Tell me what you know." He nodded toward Logan's body before his gaze roamed Charlie's jacket.

"Not a lot. I left the hospital and was walking to my car when

I found him lying on the ground. I called nine-one-one and then did my best to help him. He wasn't breathing. I checked the wound and tried to slow the bleeding but there wasn't much I could do."

"And that's why you're wearing his blood?" Shelby pointed his pen toward Charlie, his lips pursed, and his head tilted to one side.

"Ahuh."

"Care to explain how your jacket was torn?"

Charlie glanced at the tear as if noticing it for the first time. "I'm not sure," he muttered.

"It had nothing to do with the fight you had with Logan in the hospital not long before?"

"How do you know about that?" Charlie narrowed his eyes as he crossed his arms over his chest.

"We had a call."

Well, that was interesting.

Charlie scowled. "Yeah, Logan and I had a scuffle. I was visiting Daisy, and he didn't like it. He attacked me, and I defended myself."

"And then you followed him and saw an opportunity to get him out of Daisy's life for good."

"What? No!" Charlie gaped and took a large step backwards.

"He couldn't have done it, Shelby," Dorothy snapped. "He left the ward before Logan."

"Forgive me, Dorothy, but you're not the most unbiased witness in this case."

"What exactly are you saying?" She pulled herself up to her full height and planted her hands on her hips. Shelby visibly shrank under her stare as held his hands in front of his face, and unless I was mistaken there was a flash of fear in his eyes. I guessed he believed the town gossip.

"Look, I'm not trying to upset anyone," he gushed. "I'm just saying that as his mother your affections lie with your son."

"As true as that is, it doesn't make me a liar," she retaliated. "Check with the nurses at their station. They'll tell you who left first."

Shelby's shoulders dropped away from his ears as he consulted his notepad. "Then explain this to me. Charlie says he found Logan here, which indicates to me that Logan was the first to come this way. If Charlie left first, why wasn't he ahead of Logan?"

"It's because I stopped at the men's bathroom before I left," Charlie explained. "I needed to cool off and release some steam, so I went to splash some water on my face."

"And that calmed you down?" Shelby asked, scribbling in his notepad.

"Look, you know as well as I do there was no love lost between Logan and me," Charlie added. "But I didn't kill him."

Shelby licked his lips as his gaze flipped between Dorothy and Charlie. He waited a beat before asking, "Why should I be so sure you didn't wait for Logan to get ahead of you and when no one was around you killed him? Then you made it look like you stumbled across his dying body and pretended to help him."

Charlie's jaw clenched as he shook his head, his eyes lowered. "I'm not a killer. If I wanted to hurt him, I'd have Mom hit him with an incurable spell that gave him a nasty rash in places the sun doesn't shine."

Dorothy flashed a momentary grin.

Shelby sighed. "Yes, well that won't exactly stand up in court, will it?" Closing his notebook, he leaned his weight back on his heels.

"You're not seriously considering me as a suspect, are you? How do you know he wasn't a victim of a mugging?"

"Because his wallet and phone are still on his person. And as you're the one with blood on your hands, and you have a history of fighting with Logan, that puts your name at the top of my list."

"Come on!" Charlie protested.

"Shelby, you're an idiot," blasted Dorothy.

Trent Shelby shoved his hands in his pockets and eyed Charlie. "I'm sure I'll have a lot more questions for you, and if you want to prove your innocence then I suggest you be available when needed. Don't do anything to make yourself look guilty, Charlie, and don't leave town." With that, he tipped his hat in way of goodbye to Dorothy and sauntered back to the crime scene, his boots scuffing the snow.

Dorothy spun to Charlie. "Are you sure you didn't see anyone else around?"

"No. I rounded the corner, and the first thing I saw was the trail of blood on the snow. My gaze followed it, and I found Logan. Honestly, there was nothing I could have done to save him."

"Okay then." Dorothy dusted her gloves together. "We need to learn everything we can. Ana, go hang around the police and see what you can find out. Listen especially for what they think the murder weapon was. Not everyone carries a knife sharp enough to do that to a man."

My heart beat slow and heavy as I looked toward Logan. My life with him flashed before my eyes as the paramedics gave way to the coroner and he assessed the scene. Logan may not have always been honest with me, he may not have been the best fiancé, but he loved me. Knowing he died alone in the cold caused a fracture in my heart that would never repair, and I allowed the silent tears to fall.

Dorothy sniffed as she took Charlie's arm in hers. "We need to get you home so you can clean up. The sight of all that blood is making me feel unwell."

Dorothy's house was one of a kind. The high-pitched roof was enveloped in vapor as fog coiled around it. Shutters hung lose from overhead windows, and remnants of a summer garden were now lost beneath the snow blanketing her front yard. Charms and windchimes and crystals of various colors hung from her porch. Her hallway was littered with dogeared books with tantalizing titles like *The Witches Greenhouse*, *Moon Spells*, *The Psychic Witch*, and *The Encyclopedia of the World's Deadliest Plants*, and her potted herbs were growing thick and lush on the kitchen windowsill. Remnants of Christmas celebrations were scattered around the room with decorations now lacking the excitement they held a week ago.

Percival the black cat slept on the rocking chair, ignoring the yapping of Mrs. Baker's shih tzu, Clarabelle, as she defended us all against the attack of Manny, the mannequin Dorothy used to display her latest crocheted creation. This house was open to any stray, dead or alive, who needed a place to call home.

"Hi, Mrs. Baker." I half smiled at my faux grandmother who had only recently joined the afterworld. Despite us solving the mystery of who murdered her, she had not yet moved on through the channels leading to eternal peace. She said she was waiting for the day that little Clarabelle passed before she joined her husband in spirit, but personally I thought she was having more fun as a ghost than she ever did in life, so why not make the most of what she had while she had it?

"Hello, Daisy, dear. How was your visit with yourself? Any improvements? Oh dear, you look awful. Is everything okay?" She absently patted her rounded tummy tucked beneath her navy cardigan.

Charlie stomped past everyone and headed to the hallway with Ana hot on his heels.

Dorothy placed her bag on the floor, and Alfie instantly wiggled free, making his way toward Elsie, the crochet-loving friend of Dorothy.

"Well, hello, little man," Elsie cooed as she leaned to give Alfie a pat, the skin on the back of her hand wrinkled and almost translucent. As she'd spent the last ten years as a spirit, her fingers travelled through him, but it seemed he liked the gesture as he jumped onto the couch alongside her and settled in for a nap.

"Is Charlie okay?" Frank rushed forward, his brow creased. A few curly chest hairs poked from the top of his red-sequined gown, intertwining with the long lengths of his perfect beard. Long purple ringlets trailed over his shoulder, and his fake eyelashes cast eerie shadows on his cheeks. His only regret about dying in drag was that he hadn't been wearing his purple velvet gown as apparently it accentuated his contact lenses.

"He's had better days," Dorothy replied, slipping out of her boots and into her bedazzled slippers before moving straight to the liquor cabinet and pouring herself a drink.

"Oh boy. Care to tell us what's going on?"

Dorothy hurriedly recalled the events of the afternoon. By the time she'd finished, everyone looked shell-shocked, and she was pouring herself a second glass.

"I'm so sorry, Daisy," Mrs. Baker cooed, pulling a handkerchief from her sleeve and dabbing her eyes. "I never had much love for Logan, but I know you did. Are you okay?"

I had no idea how to answer that truthfully.

"It's a shock," I admitted, dragging my feet as I crossed the room to the table.

"Darling, they can't possibly think Charlie is capable of murder!" The diamonds on Frank's chubby fingers glittered as he flapped his hands around his ears, his eyes as wide as his hips.

"Calm down, Frank," warned Elsie, her spirit as vibrant as the crocheted beret she wore.

"What have I told you about calling me Frank?" he snapped, crossing his arms under his ample cleavage.

Elsie waved her hand dismissively. "I'm not calling you Frankincense. It's too much of a mouthful."

"Then can we at least agree on Frankie? It's so much cuter, don't you think?"

"Can we focus, please?" Mrs. Baker cut in, twirling her wedding ring. "Daisy's upset."

I sniffed, biting my lip as the concerned faces of my new friends stared back at me. "I'm okay," I lied.

"You don't look okay," Elsie added. "If I could fix you a brandy I would."

"I'd prefer a whiskey, but I appreciate the gesture." I gave her a weak smile.

"Are the police going to charge Charlie with murder?" Frank asked.

"They're only asking questions," Dorothy finished.

"At this stage," warned Anastasia, appearing in the room with a pop. "I saw what Shelby wrote in his notebook, and he's got Charlie pegged as suspect number one."

"Did they find the murder weapon?" Frank continued, his voice trembling. "Charlie, never touched it, did he? I was watching a rerun of *CSI* last night, and I know they'll dust it for fingerprints, so it's super important Charlie never touched it." It was common knowledge Frank had a crush on Charlie. Not that I could blame him.

"No," Anastasia added, rolling her eyes. "The police couldn't find it."

"Any information on what it could be?" Dorothy asked her.

"Something sharp." Ana shrugged.

I shivered.

"Considering we were at the hospital, and you said the murderer was wearing scrubs, then it could be a number of items."

"My guess would be a scalpel," Ana commented. "But I'm no expert, so who knows."

"What about witnesses? Were there any?"

`I slumped against the chair and bit back tears. My emotions were jumbled, and I was still in shock. Heaviness weighed on my heart, and all my energy had evaporated.

"I'm not sure. No one came forward with any names," Ana finished.

"How's Charlie dealing with it?" Elsie asked, flicking a concerned glance my way.

"He's quite shaken, and he needed to get rid of the blood, so I waited for him to get into the shower," Ana explained. "The hot water will soothe his soul and calm his nerves."

My stomach rolled, and I swallowed hard as I redirected my thoughts. "Where's Logan?"

All eyes turned to me, deep vertical lines between their brows.

"Ummm, Daisy…you were there, sweetheart," said Dorothy, moving to stand alongside me as she attempted to rub my arm. We both knew it was futile, despite me yearning for her touch. "You saw his body, so you know he's departed this Earth."

"They would have taken him to the morgue," Frank added. "It's where all bodies go."

"Yes, I know that, but what I mean is, where is he now? Why hasn't he shown up as a spirit yet?"

A collective *argh* travelled the room.

"It takes time for them to transition. The newly dead don't know the ropes and often get a bit lost. But if it helps you, I'll find Sophia and get her to search for him," said Elsie. "She's good at interpreting what the newbies are trying to say."

"Thank you. I know he was just murdered and he's having a really bad day, but turning up in the spirit world is super scary. I hate to think he's out there struggling somehow."

Charlie chose that moment to enter the room. Fresh from the shower, he wore jeans that sat low on his hips, as he pulled a t-shirt over his head. But not before we were all rewarded with the vision of his skin glistening with a fresh sheen.

Frank audibly moaned, his eyes glazing as he fanned himself. Ana stood taller as she flicked her auburn locks hair over her shoulder, and Elsie whispered something about being twenty years younger. I wanted to add she would also need to be alive, but my mind had wandered somewhere around Charlie's abdomen.

"What?" He stopped and stared back at all of us.

"Nothing!" I managed. "We were...ummm, just..." Bugger. What were we doing?

"Daisy was asking Elsie to get Sophia to find Logan," Ana gleefully chanted. She liked nothing more than putting a wedge between Charlie and me, and Logan was the biggest wedge she could get.

Charlie's gaze fell to me, and his eyes clouded with sadness.

I death-stared Ana as she smirked back at me.

"Dorothy, the spell you cast on Logan. It wouldn't have hindered his ability to fight back, would it?" I asked, turning my back on Ana.

She released a shallow breath. "It shouldn't have. It generally only lasts a few minutes, but some people do react differently to it."

"Could it have slowed his senses so he didn't even hear someone behind him?" If I could figure this out, it might make more sense to me.

"I'd think it was more that any footsteps were muffled by the fresh snowfall."

"I just don't understand who would have done that to him," I sulked.

"Did he have any enemies you know of?" Dorothy asked me.

My gaze flipped to Charlie. He caught it and gasped.

"Seriously?"

"I know you didn't do it," I huffed, rolling my eyes.

"Then why look at me when you're asked who his enemies were?"

"You're overreacting," I stated. "But you two were hardly friends."

"Yeah, and that had more to do with him than me."

It was true, but if I looked at this through Logan's eyes, then it did look like Charlie was attempting to steal his fiancée. Not that I was about to point it out.

"Don't worry Charlie," Ana purred, moving in close to his shoulder. "We know it wasn't you. Well, most of us do."

I narrowed my eyes and hit her with a glare. I was about to respond when there was a loud pop, the lights flickered, and Sophia appeared with a flash.

Frank turned wide eyes toward her, his smile reverent. "I need to learn how you do that! It's such an impressive way to enter the room."

"Yes, well everyone should know when a lady arrives," replied Sophia in her upper-class British accent, her head held high as she adjusted the row of creamy pearls strung around her wrinkled neck.

"Sophia! It's so good to see you," gushed Dorothy. "We weren't expecting you so quickly."

"Of course. I apologize for arriving unannounced, but this one turned up, screaming he needed to speak to you."

We all turned to the man who had appeared behind her. His black hood shadowed his face, his hands were shoved into the pockets of his dark jeans. He lifted his head and pulled back the hoodie, and the deep emerald-green eyes of Logan Cutter glistened back at me.

3

*L*ogan looked confused and lost, which was understandable. But he was still a whole lot more composed than I'd been when I'd woken and thought I was dead.

Sophia rolled her eyes as she released a long-suffering sigh. I had no idea why she'd been given the job of helping the newbies as she was the least tolerant spirit I knew. Not that I knew too many.

She looked down her straight nose, her fierce gaze falling to me. Her papery lips were painted red, her artificially colored curls were tucked under her felt hat, and pink blush formed two small circles on her cheeks.

"Why me?" she complained, pronouncing every syllable perfectly as she smoothed her woolen jacket and stepped toward Elsie. "I'd be far better suited to helping the gentry move on."

"The afterlife has its reasons." Elsie nodded wisely. "It's not our job to question it. And besides, this is far more interesting than hobnobbing with the rich." She grinned, and her false teeth almost popped out of her mouth. She hurriedly adjusted them and then chuckled mischievously. "I don't know why I worry about losing my teeth. It's not like they can fall on the table anymore."

"That's a blessing," added Dorothy, her grin matching Elsie's. "I can't count the number of times I've helped you pick them up."

Relief that Logan was here with us caused a sudden lightness in my soul, and I suppressed my grin as my attention momentarily flipped to Charlie, wanting everything to be okay between us.

Only he looked like Logan's appearance was causing him gas. He leaned against the counter as he held his coffee cup in a death grip. His eyes were guarded; his jaw tensed.

Oh geez.

Leaving Charlie to his thoughts, I moved across the room to Logan who'd slumped in a lounge chair. His head hung low, his expression full of torment.

"Are you okay?" I asked, kneeling in front of him, hoping I could help ease his pain. He jolted.

"Daisy? Oh, Daisy! It's good to see you!" He jumped up from the chair and flung himself toward me, his arms open wide. A chill ran up my spine as his hug travelled through my aura. His eyes widened before he wildly looked around the room.

"What…what…what's going on?" he asked, his voice shrill.

"Sophia didn't tell you?"

"Is she the old lady in the awful hat?"

I nodded.

"Well, she mentioned something about me being dead. But I… I don't feel dead. I mean, how can I be dead?" His hands moved to grab his hair.

"How do you feel?" I asked, curious.

"Vague. Like I can't quite wake up from a deep sleep and put the pieces together. But why are you here? You've woken from the coma? How did I miss that? How long have I been…dead?"

"Not long. Only hours actually. And no, I haven't yet woken up."

"I don't understand."

Well, that made two of us.

"Logan…" There was so much to tell him, but did it have to be right now? He'd had a particularly bad day, and all I wanted to do was to hold him tight and tell him everything was going to be okay—even if it was a lie. A heaviness caused my heart to beat slower and my shoulders to droop.

"Logan, sit back down." I patted the arm of the chair and held my hand out to him. "We have a lot to talk about."

"What's happening, Daisy?" His lips trembled as he looked deep into my soul for answers.

"I don't know the specifics of what happened, but earlier today someone…well, someone hurt you."

"No, you're wrong."

"You don't remember?"

He rubbed his eyes with his fists. "I remember going to the hospital to visit you but when I arrived Charlie was there." His teeth ground with the memory. "I found him kissing you," he snarled.

Everyone in the room turned to look at Charlie as the heat raced up his neck. "It wasn't like that," he growled.

Logan's head snapped toward him as if noticing him for the first time. "You're here?" He stood and faced Charlie, his shoulders pulled back, his expression dangerous.

"Considering it's my home, yeah."

I didn't add that it was technically his mother's house, and his stay was only temporary as it didn't feel productive.

"What the…?" Logan spun, scanning the room, his eyes wide. "Who are all these people?"

"It's okay," I soothed. "Calm down, and I'll explain everything."

Logan moved his eyes to mine, and it only took a moment for him to melt.

"Okay. Okay. Please tell me everything," he gushed. "And start with what the heck you're doing with him."

Oh boy. How did I begin?

"So, you remember the hospital visit?"

He nodded and started to recall the events that took place in the room. "Charlie tried to tell me he could talk to you," he scoffed.

"He could," I added, gently. "He's been able to see me for some time."

Logan's eyes were the size of saucers as his mouth formed a large O.

"Sometime after I was attacked, I woke up in his bedroom. Alfie called me there," I hurriedly added, noting the roll of hatred brewing in Logan's eyes. "And before you say anything, it's all your fault anyway. If you hadn't handed Alfie to the pound, Charlie never would have rescued him, and then we would never have met. The conversation about why exactly you surrendered my dog will be pinned for another day," I scolded, remembering how betrayed I'd felt when I'd learnt what he'd done. In hindsight I was super grateful he had.

Logan shrank back into the chair and remained quiet.

"But getting back on track, after you left the hospital today someone attacked you. Can you remember anything about it?"

He stared at the floor; his lips screwed as he rubbed his eyes. "No. Not really. I recall walking in the snow. I'd left my car in the parking lot, and I was heading there to collect it. I heard a noise behind me, and I spun to see what it was."

"Who was it?"

"No idea," he replied, shaking his head vehemently. "I don't remember anything after hearing the sound."

"What kind of sound was it?" Dorothy asked. "Footsteps? Clothes rustling?"

"Mrs. O'Leary! How, how are you?" Even in death, Logan looked scared of her.

"I'm fine, thank you. And may I say I'm sorry I put a spell on you earlier. It wasn't my preference, but you were in a mighty mood."

Logan gulped.

"Now," Dorothy continued, "do you recall what the sound was?"

"No. I'm sorry, but I...I don't know." Logan's brow was pinched, and he seemed even more transparent than he did when he arrived.

"It's okay," I said. "Why don't you have a rest? It's a lot to take in, and you might think of something when you've adjusted."

Logan looked around him, totally bewildered.

"Dorothy, do you have a spare room Logan can have a lie down in?" I asked.

"Sure. Frank, show him the way, will you?"

"Me? Why me?" Frank planted his hands on his hips.

"Because he's cute, and I thought you'd like the opportunity to spend some alone time with him." She grinned.

Frank gave Logan the once over. "Hmmm, he's no Charlie, but I guess he'll do," he mumbled.

Once Frank had led Logan from the room I turned to Sophia.

"I don't understand why he can talk to us so quickly. The others had to communicate through you until they got the hang of it."

"He's very sharp," threw in Sophia, "very quick to pick it all up. As soon as he appeared to me, I didn't have to clarify anything. It's like he's done it before."

Something about her words rang true, and a prickly feeling ran down my spine. But what was it? Logan couldn't have died before. Resurrection only happened if you were a direct descendent of God himself, and I was almost one hundred per cent sure Logan was not.

Lost in my thoughts, I was startled by movement behind me.

"Is he staying here?" Charlie gawped.

"Well, what do you suggest?" Dorothy asked. "We can hardly throw him out."

"Why can't we? Don't get me wrong, I'm sorry the guy is dead, but the last thing I want is for him to be roaming around here for eternity."

"Charlie, it could prove productive to have him here," I added.

Ana, Sophia, and Elsie were remaining silent on the subject.

Charlie slowly turned to me, his eyes dark. "Really? You want him here?"

"Well—" Oh boy. Heat raced up my neck as my mind stuttered.

"You do, don't you?" Charlie interrupted before I could get my words together.

"No, not like that. It's just…I haven't had a chance to tell him yet."

"Tell him what?"

I glanced around the room and noted how it appeared everyone was holding their breath, waiting for my reply.

"Could we talk somewhere private?" I whispered, leaning closer to Charlie. "Please."

Dorothy hurriedly picked up her crochet suddenly enthralled by her needle, as Elsie pretended to read the flyer advertising the New Year's celebrations at the town hall. Sophia looked bored as she inspected her fingernails. Ana pulled her shoulders back and scowled.

Charlie followed my gaze. "Sure. We can talk in my room."

A short while back Charlie's home had been burnt in a fire, destroying almost everything he'd owned. He was temporarily living in Dorothy's spare room until he got the insurance pay out and could find a new place to live.

As I looked at the purple velvet drapes, the multicolored

crocheted blanket covering the green sheets, and the small crystal light shade, I knew Charlie couldn't wait to get back to being surrounded by his own possessions. He'd confided in me that as much as he loved his mom, he'd spent enough years growing up engulfed by her vibrancy, and he now loved the simplicity of his own place.

I silently followed him into the room, Ana hot on our heels.

"Can we *please* have five minutes alone without her," I pleaded.

Ana dropped her perfect backside onto the bed and crossed one long leg over the other, her look defiant.

"Ana, please." Charlie's tone was sharp as a vein in his neck pulsed.

Her lip dropped, but she didn't argue. Instead, she huffed then pushed herself up and stomped from the room. Charlie closed the door firmly behind her.

"Happy?" he asked, his stare hard.

"Not exactly."

"What do you want from me, Daisy?" Stress showed in the deep crevices embedded in his forehead. I'd only known Charlie for a short time, and I never remembered those lines being quite as deep on the day I met him.

"Nothing, but it's not exactly the happiest day of my life," I confessed.

Charlie took Ana's vacant spot on the bed, his lids lowered as he stared at his hands. "I guess I can see why. The man you loved enough to want to marry just died."

"Well, yes! I am sad Logan died. Things may be different now, but I can't just stop loving him."

"Of course not. I just thought…well, it doesn't matter."

I moved to sit alongside Charlie and allowed my arm to sit close to his. His heat blasted me as sadness raced to surround my heart. Lifting my hand, I covered his and leaned in close.

"Charlie, did you stop loving Ana when she died?"

He took a moment before turning his eyes to mine. "No."

"Do you still love her, even now all that time has passed?"

"Yes, I don't think I will ever stop loving her. But it's not the same kind of love I once felt for her. Not now that I know the truth about our relationship." His gaze drifted into the space around us as a muscle quivered in his jaw.

"That she had the affair?"

"Yeah. That was a kicker."

"You seem to have forgiven her."

He turned his face toward mine. "It's complicated."

I considered him for a beat, gauging his emotions and how best to move forward. "The love you feel for Ana is what I feel for Logan. I need to tell him my feelings have changed and that the engagement was always going to be called off. But how do I do that now?"

A smile flicked at the corner of his lips. "You never mentioned to me you were going to call it off."

"Surely you'd figured it out. My heart no longer belongs to him."

"Maybe, but you've never actually said what you feel. And for who."

"Yes, well, an engaged woman doesn't go about telling other men she's falling in love with them, does she?"

"You're falling in love with me?"

Bugger. "Ummm…"

Charlie beamed, and his heat was like a furnace racing up my arm, pushing the sadness around my heart away.

"If it helps, I think I'm falling in love with you too," he whispered. His forehead stopped close to mine; our eyes locked onto one another. My heart beat an erratic tune, and butterflies zipped low in my belly. All sounds drifted into oblivion as he consumed every part of me. Something in my soul shifted, and I gasped at the intensity of it.

"I wish I could touch you," I breathed.

"You can. In here." My hand followed his as he laid it on his chest.

"It's not the same."

"I know. But this is all we have."

"I want more."

Charlie smiled lazily. "We'll have more, Daisy. Nothing and no one will stop that. I promise."

"My mom always told me not to make promises I couldn't keep."

He chuckled. "Oh, I'm going to keep this one. You wait and see. Now, come and lie with me for a while."

He pushed back on the mattress until his head was on his pillow. I moved alongside him and tucked myself against him. Resting my head on his chest, I closed my eyes, listening to his rhythmic breathing.

Only as visions of deadly nightshade wrapped themselves around my ankles, I gasped against the dread the squeezed my heart and sat up straight, snapping my eyes open.

"What's wrong?" Charlie asked, his smile slow and calming.

Taking a minute to steady myself I gulped as somewhere in the dark recess of my mind I knew the memory was important. But why did it have to resurface now—to threaten the happiness I had?

I shook myself. "Nothing," I lied, lying back down. In that moment I needed the outside world to cease to exist, because for the first time in my life, snuggled against Charlie, I felt whole, and nothing was going to steal that.

4

I wanted to spend the afternoon lying on the bed just being near Charlie, enjoying the heat travelling between us. But instead, we spent it around the dining room table surrounded by spirits all wildly talking about who killed Logan.

It was a question I couldn't ignore, especially as it seemed Charlie was the number one suspect. My heart flipped between singing a melodious tune recalling Charlie's loving words and beating slow and heavy remembering Logan's death.

"We need to solve this murder," I mused. "I think I may actually have a heart attack if we don't do it quickly."

"Oh, yay!" Mrs. Baker rubbed her hands together, delight shining in her eyes. "Does this mean the Spirit Detectives are back in business?"

I glanced around the room as the idea settled.

"That's a fantastic idea," shouted Frank, bouncing on his toes.

"How do we do it?" Charlie asked.

"Easy," Elsie added, "we make a list of suspects and then eliminate them one by one."

"That sounds harsh," Frank squealed.

"I don't mean eliminate them permanently," Elsie added with a grin. "I mean take them off the list once we've established their innocence."

Frank beamed.

"It's a good plan," Mrs. Baker added. "Where do we start?"

I shrugged. "Logan, do you remember any kind of smell before you were stabbed."

Logan sat morosely on the couch, his shoulders drooping. "Huh?" He stared into his hands, his eyes lost in another place. "What kind of smell?"

"I don't know. I just remember when I was attacked, I recalled a scent," I explained.

He screwed up his nose, looking up to the ceiling. "Yeah, now that you mention it, there was a stench. Kind of like someone passed wind. I nearly turned back and walked the long way around to the parking lot."

"Charlie, can you write some notes for me please?"

Charlie looked momentarily conflicted, but after a beat he stood and retrieved the notepad Dorothy kept on the counter near the wall phone.

"What do you need me to write?" he asked, pen poised at the ready.

"I want to make a list of everything both you and Logan can remember from the crime scene. Start with the scent."

Scratching sounded as Charlie stroked his chin, his brow wrinkled. He then scribbled what he knew. After a moment he looked at the page and grimaced.

"Read it back to me please," I asked.

"Okay. Well, Logan remembers a sound that probably wasn't footsteps and a bad smell."

"What else?"

"That's it."

"Did you add what you could recall?"

"Daisy, I don't really recall anything. I rounded the corner and saw him lying on the ground. Alone. There were footsteps in the snow, but that was to be expected considering it wasn't new snowfall and we were at a hospital. Lots of people would have walked that way. It's a busy time of year."

"You're right. So how was it no one was around at the exact time Logan got attacked?"

Charlie shrugged. "I'd guess the stench kept them away."

"But why don't you remember smelling it?" I probed.

"Because my nose was blocked after Mom's spell. I always have that reaction to it."

"Like I said earlier," chimed in Dorothy, "Charlie's been exposed to it a few too many times."

"What a strange aroma, though," added Frank.

"Yeah, and it was there before Logan arrived, which meant the attacker either had to have had an upset stomach while waiting, or the scent was there as a deterrent to others going that way, meaning there would be no witnesses to the crime."

"How would they do that?" Elsie asked, swishing her teeth backwards and forwards.

"When we were kids," Frank added, "we used to prank our schoolteachers with stink bombs." He laughed at the memory.

"Can you still buy those?" Charlie asked.

We all shrugged.

"Maybe we need to ask some kids," Frank mused.

"I know some kids who had them!" Mrs. Baker looked animated. "The Davis kids would drop them in the foyer of our building until we kept the door locked."

"That's true." I recalled the first day I'd been caught by the stench, and my stomach churned at the memory.

"It sounds lame to me." Ana smirked. "If I turned the corner and there was a bad smell, I'd just keep walking. Quickly."

"You mustn't have ever encountered any," I added.

"It was pretty bad," said Logan. "I had to put my hand over my nose to be able to breathe properly."

Silence filled the room for a beat as we all considered that.

"Logan, what else did you do today?" Dorothy asked. "If we believe this was premeditated, then the killer knew where you were going to be and when."

That was a good point.

"Who knew you were visiting me?" I asked.

Logan hesitated. "No one."

"Not very convincing," Charlie growled.

"What do you want from me?" Logan spat.

"The truth. If you want us to figure out who killed you, then some cooperation would be good."

"I never said I wanted you to solve it. Let Shelby figure it out."

"Well, I can tell you I *don't* like you here," stressed Charlie. "So if figuring this out means I'll no longer be a suspect in a murder investigation, and there's no reason for you to hang around, then I'm sure as hell going to help Shelby anyway I can!"

Logan shrank back and scowled, yet he remained quiet.

"Logan, do you like being here?" Dorothy asked.

"Not particularly. But what else am I to do?"

"Well, the good news is, once you have closure on this, it's possible you will be able to move on to a place where you'll find peace."

Logan scoffed. "Peace! What the hell is that?"

"Come on," I coaxed. "Helping us solve this will give you something to focus on. It'll help you adjust. Just ask Mrs. Baker."

"It's true," she countered. "It helped me immensely. And now I'm having the best time I've had in years. Who knew being dead could be so much fun?" She beamed.

"So true," added Frank. "I used to think being on stage was the best thing ever, but now I know scaring Patricia Watson at number thirty-two is by far the funniest thing I've ever done."

"Frank," warned Dorothy, "what have I told you about that?"

"It's not like I scare *her* exactly. It's more like her cat can see me and isn't particularly fond of a spirit sitting alongside it on the couch. When I plonk my tush, little Kitty nearly jumps out of its skin, which in turn makes Patricia spill her evening cuppa." He giggled.

Dorothy narrowed her eyes at him.

"You have to admit Patricia Watson isn't a very nice person," Mrs. Baker added. "She told Donald Pattison I caught herpes from Trevor Billings."

"Yew. Did you?" Frank grimaced.

"No! I've been nothing but faithful to my poor departed husband. She's the one who caught the herpes."

Frank looked like his Christmas's had all come at once. "You're kidding."

"Nope, she was seeing Donald behind his wife's back—"

"Okay! Fine! Please stop talking," shouted Logan, cutting Mrs. Baker off. He stood and ran his hands through his hair. "If solving my murder means I can move on and get away from you lot, then I'm in. Except you, Daisy. I never want to be anywhere but with you."

Oh boy.

Charlie glanced my way, his expression full of questions. I didn't need to ask the specifics of the questions as I was pretty sure they involved Logan and me and when I was going to tell him the engagement was off.

"So, who knew you were going to the hospital?" I trilled, doing my best to ignore Charlie.

Logan scuffed across the room and appeared to sit on the spare chair alongside me. Charlie bristled.

"I went into work at the mechanics that morning," Logan continued. "I told Mike I was visiting you, but he'd have no reason to kill me."

"I thought you were a property developer," Frank mused.

"I was. A guy can do more than one thing, can't he?" Irritation creased Logan's brow.

Memories of the relationship that Logan had with his boss

jumped to the forefront of my mind. "From what I remember you and Mike had more than one fight in the past."

"That's a lot different to killing someone."

"So did you and Mike argue recently?" Charlie asked.

"Yeah. When I told him I quit."

"What?" My eyebrows shot up to my hairline. "You just said you were broke. Why would you quit your job?"

"Because things with the development were ramping up. Amethyst had just bailed me out, and I was going to push the start button for it to begin. Someone was going to have to make sure it all went to plan."

"I heard the mechanic shop is busy at the moment. I'm guessing Mike didn't like the idea of you leaving him in the lurch."

Logan lifted a shoulder. "He wasn't overly happy, but that's no reason to kill me."

"Actually, it might be." Frank butted in.

"Why is that?" I asked, curious.

"Well, I was wandering around town last week a bit bored, and I saw the most glorious looking man enter the mechanic. I had nothing else to do so I thought I'd have a little perv." Glee twinkled in Frank's eyes. "Anyway, he may have been good to look at, but if you ask me, he was some kind of loan shark. He was demanding Mike pay him what he owed or else."

"Or else what?" Dorothy asked.

Frank used a long fingernail to feign slicing across his throat.

"But that's exactly how Logan died!" I sat heavily on the nearest chair.

"I know. What if this guy killed Logan to prove to Mike he was serious?" Frank mused.

"You've been watching too much *CSI*," Elsie added.

Charlie chewed his lip as he looked from Frank to Logan. "How much money are we talking about?"

"He said fifty thousand dollars."

Elsie let out a slow whistle. "That's a lot."

"It's definitely something we should ask Mike about," Charlie said.

"You're wasting your time," Logan spat. "I'm not that important to Mike. If someone wanted to send him a warning, they would have hurt his family."

"What if you leaving Mike threatened the business?" I asked. "Without you he wouldn't have the jobs completed in time and that would have meant he couldn't have the money ready."

"True, but I can't work while I'm dead, can I?"

I crossed my arms and bit my lip as I thought over what I knew so far. "Fair point. What happened after you and Mike had words?"

"I went…well, I just had a drive around town. I had some thinking to do and driving always clears my head."

"What was on your mind?" I asked.

"It was a…project I was working on. I needed some extra funding, and my sponsor well…they weren't available to talk to me." He picked at his fingernails absently staring at the floor.

I thought back to when I first met Charlie and how he had quoted an architectural job for Logan. "Was it the high-end offices you were building?" I probed.

Logan balked.

"I don't understand why you never told me you were going ahead with the project," I added.

"I didn't want you to know until it was complete." Logan spoke quietly, rubbing his palms together.

"Why? What was the secret? Why couldn't I know?"

He gulped. "I did ask you to be a part of the investment, but you never had any faith in me, Daisy. You always had an excuse for why it wouldn't work. I started the office project to prove you wrong. I could be a success and not the failure you see me as."

"I never thought you were a failure."

"Then why wouldn't you help me when I asked?"

"Logan, you know how I feel about the inheritance I got from my father. I'm terrified of losing the money as it'll mean all he worked for in his life would be a waste."

"But we could have doubled the money!"

"No, we would have lost it."

"What makes you so sure?" he demanded, the nearby ticking clock the only other sound in the room. Everyone appeared to be holding their breath, hanging on every syllable we uttered.

I bit my lip as I thought back over the numerous times I'd considered his proposals. "Because, well some of your ideas weren't the best."

"Name one."

"Ummm, the camera bags made from fabric spun from virgin silkworms."

"Okay that wasn't one of my best proposals."

"Neither was the knockoff Uber Eats idea," I added.

"That was a great idea!"

"Daphne's Place is the only place in town offering take away, and she already offers delivery."

Logan sighed.

"And what about the time you wanted to sell bottled water for pets?"

"What was wrong with that? Plenty of people will pay good money for their pets to have only the best!"

"Yes, but you were going to fill the bottles from the tap."

"The dogs wouldn't know the difference." Logan huffed.

"It wasn't exactly honest, was it?"

"Okay! I get your point, but the offices were different. They were a moneymaker. Lilli agreed. In fact, they were her idea."

"And we all know what kind of person she is," I finished quietly.

Logan dropped his head into his hands, his shoulders curled forward. "I'm sorry, Daisy. I really am. Lilli wanted me to keep it all a secret from you from the get-go. I should have known not to listen to her."

I exhaled loudly. "Don't worry about it." Unable to look at him, I stood and moved across the room, Alfie hot on my heels. I didn't want to hold a grudge against Logan for being taken in by Lilli, but if I were being honest with myself, I had felt betrayed when I'd learned of their corporate union.

I absently stared at an old photo of Charlie in a Boy Scout uniform, holding a new badge, his chest puffed and his smile large. I lifted my hand to the frame, wishing I could run my finger over the glass as my thoughts raced. "Logan, did you say the offices were Lilli's idea?" I spun to face him, my brow pinched.

"Yes. I wanted to buy one on the other side of the park, but she was specific about it being that one. She said if she was putting up the money then she should get a say."

"So, you two were in partnership?"

"No. She just funded it, but no one was to know."

"I don't understand." I shook my head, willing the pieces to click into place. "Why didn't she want her name on it? And why that specific building?"

He shrugged. "I didn't question it."

Charlie stood and moved toward me. "What are you thinking?"

"I'm not sure, but it sounds really odd. When Logan originally approached me about the money, I spoke to Lilli. She was the one who was opposed to it stating how it wasn't a good business idea —this town is far too small for such expensive offices and how many do we have already vacant? She specifically told me my dad wouldn't approve of me investing in it and talked me out of even considering the offer. So why would she then turn around, give Logan the money, and then specify it had to be that exact site?"

"It's a good question," Charlie mused. "Any ideas, Logan?"

Logan shook his head. "I never questioned her. Not after the night I had a dream about it."

"You dreamt about it?" My head shot up as I stared at him.

"Yeah. That day you and I had argued about it, so I told Lilli I was pulling out of the project. She wasn't happy and told me to go home and sleep on it. That night I had a dream, and in it the offices were awesome. Walls of gleaming glass with views over the pond, plush carpets, high ceilings, and walls of polished concrete. The mayor was congratulating me on bringing such quality to the town. You were proud of me, Daisy."

I swallowed hard. "Oh no. Lilli did that. She planted the dream. What I want to know is—why?"

5

ogan laughed humorlessly. "Daisy, I think that knock to the head killed a few brain cells."

"What?" I demanded, my eyes narrow.

"How do you think Lilli planted a dream in my head?"

"She's a night demon." I crossed my arms over my chest as I considered Logan. "But I think you already know that."

He looked away, scuffing the toe of his sneaker on the floor. "There's no such thing."

I moved to stand in front of him, needing to see his eyes—only they were guarded, the shutter to his soul slammed closed.

"What are you not telling me?" I asked.

"Nothing. You know what I know," he replied, his emerald-green depths turning darker.

I sat back on my heels and took a few deep breaths. Even though I didn't want to be privy to the secrets people kept in their sleep, I occasionally created a dream for them where I could communicate. And I was slowly learning I could even do that in their daydreams. If I was to connect with the secrets Logan was hiding, this seemed like the best way to do it. I closed my eyes and focused on Logan, wanting to take him to a place that only the two of us knew.

Come on, show me what you know.

But his walls were up, preventing me from getting close.

"Why won't you let me in?" I asked, snapping my eyes open and stomping my foot.

"I'm not stopping you," he responded, a muscle in his jaw clenching.

"So, you know what I'm trying to do." Why wasn't I surprised he knew?

He shrugged.

"Logan, tell me what's going on." My tone was hard even to my own ears.

"Nothing is going on!" He hurriedly stood and stared at me.

"You know both Lilli and I are night demons." It was more a statement than a question. "How long have you known?"

He shrugged nonchalantly, licking his lips as his gaze dropped to the floor. "I didn't know anything for sure. I'd heard rumors around town about such beings but never believed it. It was only when you fell into a coma and I no longer slept alongside you my dreams turned to nightmares. That's when I started to wonder." He gave me a sidelong glance as he slipped his hands into his hoodie pockets.

My scalp prickled, and my stomach quivered. Logan was a bad liar. I just didn't understand why he was lying to me now.

"Daisy." Charlie stepped in alongside me. "Why don't we head over to the offices and have a look around. We might learn something about why Lilli wanted Logan to buy it."

"Do you think it's related?" Dorothy asked.

Charlie shrugged.

I didn't care. An outing sounded like a good idea and might just clear my head. I glared at Logan, but as Charlie smiled all my pent-up frustration dissolved.

"Wait for me," called Ana, tottering on her Louboutin heels behind us.

"And me," Logan added, his shoulders tensed.

Charlie released an exasperated breath as he grabbed a new jacket from the hook and pushed his arms into the sleeves.

"Do we need a parade?" he asked.

"I have every right to go. It's my building," spat Logan. "Well… it was."

I stared at him, my eyebrows raised.

"I haven't made the last few payments to the bank, and they were going to take control of it."

"I thought Lilli was funding you with my money?" I queried.

Logan looked like he'd been slapped. His chest deflated, and his voice became quiet. "I didn't know Lilli was stealing from you."

Did I believe him? Memories of all the times I'd learned Logan had lied to me zipped through my mind, but none of them compared to this. I felt betrayed by his actions with Lilli and learning that he'd done it all with my stolen money stabbed me in the heart. But I also knew Lilli and what she was capable of. If she'd controlled him through his nightmares, then I could see how he'd been caught up in something he had no say in. It didn't alleviate his guilt, but it helped me come to terms with it.

Charlie stepped between us, breaking our connection and any chance I had of seeing the truth hidden in the depths of his soul. "Why didn't Lilli give you the rest of the money you needed?"

"The money ceased when she was arrested recently. And I, ummm, don't have enough to finish what I started."

I sighed. "So, can we get access? Or will the bank have it locked?"

"The bank doesn't own it. Lilli's mother, Amethyst, has taken over her financials, and she paid the outstanding amounts."

My heart stuttered, and my eyes bugged as I stared back at him.

"So Amethyst Alexander is now the owner of your office building?"

A chill raced through me. Amethyst Alexander was not a nice woman. She was head of the local coven of night demons, and I'd seen first-hand what happened to those she controlled.

"Ummm, not exactly." Logan fidgeted uncomfortably.

"Care to elaborate?"

"It's still in my name, but we have an agreement."

I planted my hands on my hips and narrowed my eyes. Logan shuffled from one foot to the other.

"Why would she do that?" Charlie asked.

Logan lifted one shoulder; his lips pressed together.

"When did all of this happen?" I asked.

"Yesterday. She came to me at home with the offer to bail me out."

"And what did you have to give her in exchange? Your soul?" I berated.

Logan gulped and shrunk into the folds of his hoodie.

"What's so special about that building?" Charlie asked.

"I don't know," Logan whispered. "Everyone was adamant it had to be that one, and as they were paying for something I wanted, I went along with it."

Charlie clenched his fist as he slowly shook his head. "It's time to start asking those questions."

Dandelion Ponds was made up of a small pocket of houses all wrapped around three different sized ponds. The houses were painted in various colors that brightened a dull winter's day, yards were kept tidy, and chimneys billowed smoke. Today a handful of residents were out in the park readying it for the New Year's celebrations. The larger than average Christmas tree now decorated with a dusting of snow still held pride of place, its baubles twinkling with fairy lights, and unlit streetlights were swathed in red bows. Checking the church clock as we passed it, I knew daylight would quickly fade, and those streetlamps would soon illuminate warm pools of light.

The Mustang engine roared as Charlie navigated our way across town. Melted snow hit the underside of the vehicle as grey sky threatened to dump more snow on Dandelion Ponds. I loved fresh snow, but I hated icy roads and the mess left as it all melted. But not for the first time since waking as a spirit was I wishing I could feel the freezing air as it chilled me to the bone. I promised myself when I woke, I would never complain about a dreary winter's day again.

"I can't believe it's New Year's Eve tomorrow," I mused. "I was really hoping I'd be awake to enjoy the fireworks. It's my favorite part of the season."

"Maybe you will be." Charlie smiled and turned into the business hub being developed in the center of town—if you could call new council chambers, two office buildings, and a recreation center a hub.

As construction had been halted for the week between Christmas and New Year, buildings in varying degrees of completion loomed dark and haunting. Machinery sat quiet, dumpsters sat empty, and plastic tarps covered steel beams. Charlie pulled into a marked parking space on the side of the road and killed the motor.

"It looks pretty deserted," I commented.

"All the better for us to snoop around it then." He grinned.

Pushing the car door open, he stepped into the cold, his breath hanging in vapor around him. After giving us time to all climb out, he closed the door and locked the car behind us.

Single file, Charlie led the way along the path lined with graffitied walls, the large swirly pattern vibrant against the dull grey façade. The main entrance door was ajar, so he pushed it aside, and we all made our way along the corridor and into the cavernous room that was Logan's.

Cement walls rose high above us, electrical wires hanging from metal ceiling batons. Large glass windows framed the view of the neighboring allotments half buried in snow. Other than two chairs in the center of the room, it was empty.

"Not exactly spectacular," Ana commented, her gaze travelling the space.

"It would have been if I could have finished it," Logan replied with a smile. "I was going to have living walls, plush carpets, and only the best finishes."

"Living walls?" Ana asked him, her perfect brow slightly furrowed.

"Yeah, full of plants. Floor to ceiling." Logan started to explain the various greenery he was going to display, but I allowed their conversation to fall into the background as I wandered to the farthest corner of the room.

"Getting any vibes?" Charlie asked, behind me. "Anything to tell you why the Alexander family wanted this particular block?"

Turning my back to the wall I tried to ignore the small tremor that rippled through me. I'd been in this building before, so why now was I feeling trapped? Was I having a reaction to knowing how Logan had lied to me about it? Or was it something much more fearful?

A memory stirred, tantalizing me as it sat just out of my reach. It was important. I just didn't know why.

I looked at Charlie, refocusing with the desire to solve the puzzle. "What I don't understand is, if this building is significant, then why didn't Lilli just buy it herself? She had the money, so she didn't need to take mine, nor did she need Logan's involvement."

"You're asking the wrong person that question. I didn't even know who the Alexanders were before moving here."

"Charlie when you did up the proposal for Logan, did you

learn what this piece of land was used for prior to this development?"

He shook his head. "Do you know?"

"No. It's been vacant for as long as I can remember."

"I can do some digging and find out if you think it's relevant."

"It might not hurt to know," I said, reaching toward a fernlike seedling pushing up through a crack in the subfloor. It looked familiar, but I couldn't remember why.

Charlie pulled out his phone and tapped some notes into an app.

"You know, Charlie, I think being here is a waste of time. Amethyst already purchased the building from Logan, so why would she kill him over it?"

We glanced toward Logan as he animatedly explained to Ana how he was going to transform the area. Her expression was glazed, so I was unsure if she was enjoying it or not.

"Did he have a will?" Charlie asked me.

I nodded. "Yes. Lilli had both of us draw one up when we got engaged."

"Who would benefit from his death?"

"Me. But we all know I didn't kill him."

"Who was next in line?"

I shrugged. "He never told me, and I never thought to ask. I honestly thought I'd have at least another sixty years of living to do."

Charlie added the question to his list while I listened as Logan painted a mental picture of his dreams.

"Do you think there's potential for this to be lucrative like Logan believes?" I whispered to Charlie.

"No. I didn't even when he asked me to quote the job. Don't get me wrong, his vision was great. The finished product would have been amazing, but this town has no need for it. I suggested he lower the specifications to reduce costs, and then maybe he could have made a profit. But honestly, Daisy, there's a lot of work to be done here. The benefit would have to have been worth the effort."

"I can see why he was dazzled by the idea. He always fancied himself something much more highbrow than a mechanic, which was why he kept thinking up so many business ideas. But Lilli was a lawyer. She was smart. I could see her funding it to support him as she always had a soft spot for Logan. But why did she tell me not to?"

Charlie's brow pinched as he tapped my thoughts into his phone. As he hit save, he looked up at me ready to say something when crunching underfoot echoed from the entrance.

We both spun toward the noise as Ana and Logan fell silent.

"Charlie O'Sullivan." Officer Trent Shelby stepped over the threshold and into the room.

"What are you doing here?" Charlie asked him.

"I was about to ask you the same question."

"Ummm…" Charlie glanced my way, his eyebrows raised.

"I don't know what to tell him," I added, glad Shelby couldn't see me, Logan, or Ana.

Shelby never waited for an explanation. "This morning I find you standing over the dead body of Logan Cutter, his blood smeared all over your jacket, and now I find you trespassing on his property."

"Technically it's not his," Charlie answered.

"Care to explain?" Shelby's rubber soled shoes were quiet on the concrete floor as he moved closer to Charlie.

"I heard Amethyst Alexander bought him out."

Shelby looked surprised. "How do you know that?"

"Ummm…" He could hardly say Logan told him.

"Tell him you heard a rumor," I threw in, glaring at Logan to help him out.

Logan leaned back on his heels and grinned.

Urgh!

"Overheard someone talking about it at the bar," Charlie elaborated.

"Doesn't explain what you're doing here."

"I was curious about why she would want it. Anyway, what are you doing here?"

"I was driving by and saw your car out the front. Wondered if it was connected to why you killed Logan."

Charlie gritted his teeth. "I didn't do it."

"We'll see after I interview some witnesses to the crime. Now, care to fill me in on the real reason you're here." Only a short while ago Shelby and Charlie had come to some kind of kinship. Today it looked strained.

Charlie sighed. "Look, it strikes me as odd the Alexanders would want the building."

"Maybe they think it's a good business proposition," Shelby added.

"Do you?"

Shelby's shoulders sagged slightly as his grin exploded. "No. I don't. But then it's not my money, is it?"

"So, the day after they pay all outstanding debts, Logan is killed."

"What are you suggesting?"

"That it's connected."

Shelby pursed his lips as he stared at Charlie. "Then why would they kill him?"

"Maybe Logan didn't step away from the project willingly."

Charlie flicked a glance my way as I spun toward Logan.

"Did you?" I asked him. "Did it all go down amicably?"

"No, but what choice did I have?" Logan explained.

"What do you mean?"

"I told her I didn't want to give the project up. It was in my name, and I wanted to see it to completion. But Amethyst was calling the shots when it came to Lilli's money and said the only way I wouldn't go bankrupt was if she paid the outstanding balance. She's a scary woman when she wants something."

"Did she threaten you?"

"Every syllable she spits out sounds threatening," he finished, looking defeated.

"Shelby," Charlie cut in. "I heard Logan didn't sign it over willingly. Amethyst threatened him."

A slight stretch, but it was interesting to see where he was going with it.

"I'm having a hard time believing Amethyst Alexander wanted to pay for it for any reason other than honoring Lilli's financial commitments," Shelby protested. "But I'll look into it. In the meantime, I suggest you go home and stop trespassing. And be available, as I'm undoubtedly going to have more questions for you. Now, I'll follow you out, shall I?"

It was more of an order than a question, so Charlie did as asked and led the way to the Mustang, followed closely by Shelby.

It was only after Shelby got into his police vehicle and powered off down the road that Charlie unlocked the door. Ana and Logan piled into the back seat, but just as I was ready to follow them, a flash of red caught my eye.

On the far side of the building a woman with her head down ran toward a waiting car, her knee-high Italian leather boots imprinting the snow. She looked familiar. But it couldn't be…

"Follow her!" I demanded.

"Why?"

"Because she was spying on you."

"You're sure?"

"Yes!" No. Maybe. "She had to be."

"Daisy, we don't even know who she is."

"It looked like Lilli," I added.

"She's behind bars."

"No, she's out on bail," Logan cut in. "But she wouldn't be here."

"What makes you so sure?" I asked.

"She wouldn't lurk around like that."

He was right. As a lawyer Lilli had intimidating people down to an art. The only reason she would hang in the background was if she could learn something.

"Whatever the reason is, she's getting away," said Ana leaning over Charlie's shoulder.

Charlie narrowed his eyes as the woman's car sped in the opposite direction. "I guess so, but there's a thousand innocent possibilities of why she was here."

"And if they were innocent, why did she run?" I placed my hands on my hips and dared him to argue.

Charlie released an agonized breath. "What do you want me to do?"

"I want you to follow her."

"Don't worry about it," Ana added, rolling her eyes. "I'll follow her and see what she's up to." With that she disappeared with a pop.

"Now what?" Logan asked.

"Now we go home and wait for Ana to report back to us."

6

It didn't take Ana long, and she caught up with us just as Charlie pulled the Mustang to a stop outside of Dorothy's house. She landed in the car almost sitting on Logan's knee.

"Oh dear. So sorry," she cried, yet the upturned corners of her lips told me she wasn't sorry at all. "I thought you'd be sitting behind Charlie. My bad."

"It's not a problem," Logan replied, his color a whole lot better than it had been since he'd arrived as a ghost.

"I'd better get off," Ana continued, wiggling her backside until she was on the seat alongside him. For a ghost who could pop in and out whenever she wanted, she sure did it slowly.

"What did you learn?" Charlie asked, his scowl firmly in place.

"Not a lot," Ana said, grinning at Logan as she fiddled with the ends of her hair. "She headed to the bar, but I lost her in the crowd."

"How?"

Ana glared at me. "The bar is extremely crowded at the moment. There seems to be some kind of fancy dress party going on, and I lost her amongst the fifty women all wanting a drink."

"So, it was a complete waste of time," I complained.

"Not exactly." Ana smirked. "Before I lost her, she made a phone call. I just don't know who she was talking to, but the topic of conversation was interesting."

"Was it Lilli?" I asked.

"What does she look like?" Ana shot back.

"Dark hair, grey eyes, and legs that go on forever."

"Then, no. It wasn't her."

"What did she look like?" I pushed, disappointment weighing my stomach.

"I'm not sure. She kept her eyes hidden behind dark glasses, and I'm positive she was wearing a wig, which is how I lost sight of her amongst the partygoers."

"The how do you know it wasn't Lilli?"

"Because this woman was height challenged."

"Oh, okay."

"What was the phone conversation about?" Charlie asked.

"She was giving instructions to someone about where she left a fresh security guard uniform, along with a fake badge. Once dressed, whoever she was talking to was to make their way up to the third floor and get what she needed."

"Which was?"

"I have no idea. She never specified, and I gathered the person she was talking to already knew what his or her mission was. The call was more about the location of where they would find the disguise."

I cocked my eyebrow and tilted my head at Ana, silently asking for more information.

"Level three, locker twenty-three," Ana continued, rolling her eyes in my direction. "It was going to be left unlocked."

I sighed. "Did you learn when they were going to do whatever it is they're supposed to do?"

"Ahuh. They're on the way there now."

"Great. So, all we have to do is go to an unspecified location, make our way to the third floor, and locate some unidentified person in a security guard uniform," added Charlie, his shoulders slumping.

"That's the gist of it."

"She had to be talking about the hospital," I explained. "It's the only building around here with that many levels."

"Once we're there, how do we know if we've found the correct security guard? The hospital is crawling with them." Logan's gaze fell to Ana.

"I guess we'll figure that out as we go." She shrugged.

"They'll probably be the one opening locker twenty-three," I added.

"Is this worth following up?" Charlie seemed to be talking more to himself than us as he tapped the screen of his phone. Looking over his shoulder, I skimmed his growing list of notes.

"The call sounded very covert," Ana continued.

"And you're sure she wasn't talking to one of the women in fancy dress?"

"As sure as I can be."

"Adding that this woman hadn't made herself known to us at the office building, I think it's worth at least taking the time to find out what she's up to," I finished.

Charlie pushed his phone into his pocket and looked around our group. He shrugged. "I guess it's not like we have anything else constructive to do."

The Dandelion Ponds Regional Hospital wasn't huge, but it was in the catchment area of four adjoining towns, which meant it was the only facility in an area of about five hundred square miles. It had two small operating theaters, an emergency room, and a helicopter pad on the roof.

The holiday season was usually a busy time, and today was no exception. The entrance doors swished open and closed as visitors bustled about their day. A cleaner had the full-time job of keeping the floors clean and dry from the snow being carried in on every foot, and the security guard on the door looked like he was wishing it was the end of his shift.

We all silently followed Charlie, making our way past the coffee shop where a handful of nurses sat for a much-needed break. A man in a hospital gown pulled his IV trolley toward the door, an unlit cigarette clamped between his fingers, and two doctors stood with their heads bent over some papers discussing a condition I prayed I would never catch.

"The elevator is down the corridor on the left," I whispered.

Charlie pulled his phone from his pocket and put it to his ear, pretending to speak into it. "First of all, I know exactly where the elevator is as I visit you at least once a day. And secondly, why are you whispering?" The corners of his lips turned up ever so slightly.

"Habit. Sometimes I forget no one else can see or hear me." I grinned.

"You two better hurry up," Ana called over her shoulder as she scurried ahead of us. "The phone call was already twenty minutes ago. We don't even know who we're looking for, and time is of the essence."

Charlie picked up his pace. "Ana, can you go ahead and see what you can find?"

She huffed. "Really? You know Charlie I'm not your errand boy."

He flashed her an apologetic grin. "Sorry. I didn't mean to make you feel that way. But you have the skills to get the job done, and I know that I can rely on you."

She rolled her eyes. "Fine." With that she disappeared with a pop. I would have been envious of the whole spirit thing if I weren't hoping to wake up soon. As it stood, I lacked the abilities of normal spirits.

The elevator swished open, and Logan and I followed Charlie in as he pressed a button to a level not marked for public use. Pan pipes echoed quietly from speakers hidden inside the elevator, its purpose to calm all of those within its walls. Today, it had no effect on me. I was anxious, and I didn't think any amount of music would fix that, and as the door opened to the third floor, I dashed out hoping to see Ana waiting for us.

"There she is," whispered Charlie as he pointed to the far end of the brightly lit hallway. "She's waving us that way."

"What's this floor used for?" Logan asked as we all made our way toward her.

I allowed my gaze to roam, noting stainless steel frames holding fabric baskets filled with linen, three abandoned wheelchairs, and a trolley of medical equipment pushed against the wall.

Charlie indicated he wanted to remain silent, but as no one could hear Logan and me we continued to discuss the uses of the floor. Poking our heads into a few rooms, we quickly decided it was a service area.

Reaching a t-section, Charlie turned right, and it only took a moment for us to see Ana pointing to a man using a security pass to exit the area.

Charlie ran down the corridor toward him, but the door closed locking us on the wrong side.

Urgh!

"Was he the guy we were looking for?" I asked.

"He's dressed that way," replied Logan following me as we made our way closer. "Only it's weird he was carrying a bunch of flowers."

"He could have been a legitimate guard and is heading off to meet his girlfriend for lunch," Charlie mused.

"No." Ana shook her head. "I followed him from locker twenty-three and into that room." She nodded to a door on her left.

We all turned to it, and I noted the sign marked *Security*.

"Is it locked?" I asked.

Charlie glanced behind him before trying the handle. He nodded.

"So, who was he?"

Ana narrowed her eyes in my direction. "Do I look like a mind reader to you?"

"I want to know what he was doing in there," Charlie stated.

Ana shrugged. "I'm no computer expert, but he was tapping on a lot of keys. He obviously hit the jackpot when he sat back and smiled."

"Okay, can you follow him? I want to know who he's working for and what exactly he was looking for."

She pouted. "Why do I have to be the one who's always popping off? Can't I stay and have some fun here." Her gaze momentarily flipped to Logan.

Charlie turned and looked her in the eye. "Please."

She huffed. "Oh, all right. But this is seriously the last time I'm following some strange man around a hospital." With that she disappeared with a pop.

"We need to get in there," Charlie continued once Ana had gone.

"Really? Why? Do you know your way around the computer to figure out what he was doing?" I knew I had no idea.

"Not really, but he might have left something open that will give us a clue as to what the woman wanted from him." Charlie shrugged.

"Someone's coming," Logan hissed.

I spun to see who it was and noted the black uniform of a security guard, his steps long and purposeful, his gaze locked onto Charlie.

"Can I help you?" His eyes narrowed, and a deep vertical crease marred his otherwise gorgeous face.

"I, ummm, I think I'm lost," Charlie lied, his gaze searching the corridor. "I was looking for the men's bathroom."

The guard tipped his head back the way he came, and some of his blond locks fell over his eye. "This floor isn't for the public."

"Is this level four?" Charlie asked, feigning innocence.

"No. Three."

"Silly me. I got off a floor too soon."

The guard laughed good heartedly. "You wouldn't be the first to do that."

"So sorry to have bothered you." Charlie smiled, but as the guard turned his back and opened the door to the security room, Charlie tilted his head indicating we should get in there for a look around.

I didn't need to be told twice. The second there was a gap I could squeeze through, I was in, Logan right alongside me.

The interior of the room was dark after being in such a brightly lit hallway. A desk was pushed along one wall, a bank of monitors behind it displaying the hospital from every angle. Computers sat on the desktop, their screens filled with files, and another guard slumped forward in his chair, head on the desk. His gentle snores filled the silence.

"Looks like this is the eyes of the place," Logan commented, bypassing the sleeping man and surveying the screens that lit the room.

"Hey, Dwayne!" The guard nudged his sleeping friend. "You better not get caught napping on the job. The boss doesn't take too kindly to that."

Dwayne stirred, slowly sitting up and rubbing his face, before glancing around him, confusion in his eyes.

"What the heck, Andy?" he croaked. "Was I asleep?"

"Out like a light."

"But, but…I've never fallen asleep on the job before."

"What's that smell in here?" Andy asked, his nose tilting as he inhaled deeply. "It's making me feel sleepy."

"I bet it's valerian." I took a guess, wishing someone would describe the scent so I could verify it.

"Why do you say that?" Logan asked.

"That fake guard"—I used my fingers to air quote—"was carrying flowers. Valerian is a plant known to make you sleep. I'm guessing he used it against this guy. Once he was asleep, the intruder would have access to whatever he needed in here."

Dwayne rubbed his shoulders before turning back to the computer screen in front of him. He scrolled around a few files and then leaned back, scratching his head, his brow creased.

"What's wrong?" Andy asked.

"It's weird, but I have yesterday's CCTV backup files open. I don't remember doing that. Andy, I think I'm losing my mind."

"Maybe you should go for a break. Get some fresh air."

Logan moved in to scan the screen, his eyes wide.

"Yeah, maybe I should." Dwayne rolled his chair back, stood, and made his way to the door.

"Logan, we'd better follow him before we're stuck in here."

As Logan hadn't yet mastered the finer points of being a spirit and I lacked all abilities, it seemed like a good opportunity.

We both hurried after the guard, making our escape just in time.

"What did you see?" I asked Logan as Dwayne scuffed his way toward the corridor, yawning.

"Lots of dated files."

"Why would an unknown woman get a male friend to dress as a guard and then break into the security room to look at backup files?" I asked, as Ana suddenly reappeared.

"What did I miss?" she asked, her attention solely on Logan. He hurriedly brought her up to date.

"Hmmm." Her full lips pursed as she considered the information. "I think the fake guard was looking to remove some evidence," Ana replied, "evidence of someone committing murder, maybe."

"What did you learn by following him?" I asked.

"He was young. Looked like a high school kid to me. Harry Potter glasses, and a 'World of Warcraft' t-shirt under the guard uniform." She shrugged. "I know I shouldn't judge, but I know a computer nerd when I see one, and my guess is the kid was accessing the security records to remove CCTV evidence."

I chewed my lip and thought over what we knew. Ana had a good point. If the woman we'd seen at the office building was our killer, then she would need the footage of her in the act of murdering Logan removed before anyone could see it.

"Could the kid be our killer?" I asked.

"I've never seen him before in my life," Logan added.

"I think the woman he's working for is our killer," Ana stated.

"But why would the kid remove evidence for her?" Logan asked her.

"Maybe he didn't know he was removing it. We don't know for sure what he was doing in there. He could have been planting a computer virus for all we know." Ana parked her hand on her hip.

"If it's the CCTV footage they were after, surely the police would have taken a copy by now." I bit my lip and considered what we knew. "So, what purpose would there be to erase it here?"

Ana rolled her eyes. "Daisy, do I look like a detective to you? How would I know?"

"I think the police station should be our next stop," Logan finished, stepping between us.

"And then what?" I asked.

"Charlie can ask Shelby if he has a copy and what it showed."

My sigh matched Ana's. "Charlie can't do that. What's he going to tell Shelby—he was snooping at the hospital and saw a kid dressed as a fake guard in the security room? A kid who Ana probably can't pick in a line of teenagers all wearing 'Warcraft' t-shirts."

"Then what do you suggest?" Logan barked.

"I think the fact the kid had the valerian, makes it pretty clear he was working for Lilli," I mused.

"I've told you before, Daisy, it wasn't Lilli," Logan huffed.

As if I were taking his word for that.

"How can we find out for sure?" I asked.

"We could get Charlie in there to check the computer history," Ana suggested. "But as his guardian angel I don't like that idea very much. There's a high risk he'd get caught as I'm not sure Charlie would know his way around that system. He could be there for hours trying to find what we're looking for."

"If I wait long enough for the guards to fall asleep, maybe I can influence one of them to open the file for us," I suggested.

"How long would that take?" Logan asked.

"After the large coffee he was inhaling, it'd probably be hours."

"What else can we do?" Ana asked.

"What about getting some of those flowers the fake guard used?" Logan suggested.

"Good idea. But valerian of that quality isn't common. You would have to know where it was being grown to find some."

"So where in Dandelion Ponds would it be growing?" Ana asked. "If that guy had some, then it has to be available."

"There's only one place I know where it could be, and I for one don't want Charlie anywhere near it."

"And where is that?"

"In the greenhouse belonging to Amethyst Alexander."

7

───────

We found Charlie in Ward Four-B sitting on the chair alongside my bed.

My monitors still beeped steadily, the oxygen being fed to me through my nasal tube was still whooshing, and I still slept, seemingly without a care in the world.

"You'd think they'd pluck those eyebrows for you," Ana commented looking down at me.

"It's the first thing I'm going to do when I get out of here," I replied, self-consciously rubbing my brow.

Logan leaned his back against the wall looking paler than I'd ever seen him.

"What did you find?" Charlie asked Ana.

She hurriedly brought him up to date as I studied myself. It was like looking in a mirror but not recognizing the person staring back at you.

"Will you remember all of this when you wake up?" Logan asked, his gaze copying mine.

I bit my lip as I glanced at Charlie. "I hope so."

Logan's shoulders dropped. "I guess I'll no longer be there for you when the time comes."

"What do you mean?"

"We planned on getting married in the summer. Being your husband, I would have always been there for you, but now I'm...well..." He lowered his gaze, inspecting his arms and hands and taking in his overall appearance. His shoulders sagged.

"I'll be all right, Logan. You don't have to worry about me."

"Daisy, I know you think what I did with Lilli was wrong, and I'm so sorry I wasn't honest with you about it."

"I can understand why you did it. She's a powerful woman."

"So, you forgive me?" Pain radiated from within the depths of his eyes.

"One thing this whole situation has taught me is to no longer hold grudges. None of us know when our clock will stop ticking, so why waste the moments we have being upset over something we can't change—some good advice Grandpa once gave me," I explained with a small smile.

Logan nodded repeatedly as a weak smile broke through his agony. His lips moved soundlessly as he seemed to struggle for words.

"I wish we'd had more time together," he finally managed, his hand reaching out to mine. "If I could change all of this, I would hold you forever and never let you go."

I gulped and stared at my sleeping self, unable to return his gaze.

"Logan, there's something we need to talk about," I whispered, not wanting to say the words, but knowing they had to be said. "It's about Charlie..."

"Daisy, stop! Please don't say it," he begged. "Not yet."

"But..."

"Please. I need to hold onto something to get through all of this."

I swallowed hard and nodded, pushing down the feeling of guilt threatening to smother me.

To distract myself, I allowed my focus to drift back to Charlie and Ana and the conversation they were having.

"So, you think that's what the fake guard was doing? Destroying evidence?" Charlie confirmed.

"He knew what he was looking for, and he knew how to navigate the system easily." Ana nodded.

"If he's destroyed the footage, then we'll never know the truth of who killed me." Logan sulked.

"Don't give up hope," I encouraged. "There'll be other ways to figure it out. In fact, I've been thinking about it. Surely Officer Shelby has copies of the files by now. And if so, he'll see who did it and will be arresting them before the day is out." I was ever hopeful.

"That's a good point, Daisy," Charlie mused. "And if you're right, then we should go and have a chat with him."

I was about to respond when the door opened behind me. I spun on my heel as nurse Amanda crossed the room toward my bed.

"Hello, Charlie. I thought I heard someone talking to Daisy."

"I believe it's good for her," he replied, stepping back and allowing her access to my monitors.

"It seems you're good for her. Whenever you're here, Daisy's response is amazing." She tapped at the digital screen and smiled.

Logan scowled.

Charlie flicked a glance my way.

"Is she showing any more signs of waking up?" he asked Amanda.

"Yes. While her mom, Maggie, and her grandpa were here this morning Daisy fluttered her eyelids."

Despite my strained relationship with my family I would have enjoyed that visit, and I wished I knew what happened to my body when my spirit wasn't around.

"She would have been excited with Daisy's response," Charlie added.

"She was. No matter how old we get, our moms never stop worrying about us."

"What happens now? With Daisy?"

"We're waiting on the specialist to run a few more tests. We'll know more then, but we're talking about removing her breathing tubes."

"That's great news."

"It really is…even though a lot has happened while she's been asleep. I'm worried about how she'll take the news of her fiancé passing."

"She's got a good support system around her," Charlie added.

Amanda nodded. "It was awful though, right? Him being killed on hospital property—I mean, this is a place where we try to save lives. Not take them."

"Small town like this, I guess everyone would know Logan in some capacity."

"Yeah. He seemed like a really nice guy who truly loved her."

Charlie flinched. "I'm sure she'll be devastated, but like I said. She has a good support system."

Amanda glanced over her shoulder, biting her lip. "You're not thinking of her family, are you? It's just that I know you haven't been in town for long and probably don't know them well, but they haven't exactly been a pillar of strength for Daisy. Her grandpa visits regularly, and her mom pops in when she can, but the rest of them hardly ever come to visit her. I can't imagine their being the support she needs when she wakes up."

Charlie gave her a small smile. "It's okay. Daisy has me and my mom to help her. Plus, a lot of good friends. We'll give her everything she needs."

Amanda's shoulders relaxed as she adjusted the pillow behind my head. "That's good. She deserves only the best."

"Did you know her well before the attack?" Charlie asked.

"No, not really. I didn't grow up in Dandelion Ponds. I only moved here a few months ago, but from what I've been told Daisy has a kind soul."

My heart swelled with her words, and I made a mental note that once I woke, I would always send flowers to the ward in way of thanks for everything they had done for me.

***

Dandelion Ponds' one and only police station was located on the corner of Aurora Drive and Luna Avenue. It was housed in a square two-story brown brick building with a public area at the front and two holding cells at the back. Two of its three resident police officers were Trent Shelby, and the pretty new recruit in the shiny uniform who beamed at Charlie from behind the counter.

Crossing the vinyl floor, past the four plastic chairs pushed against the wall and the small table holding a tree displaying the remnants of Christmas, Charlie lifted his hand in way of a greeting.

As the officer's gaze fell to him, her shoulders straightened. She flicked her long blonde ponytail over her shoulder, her fake eyelashes hitting her bangs as her eyelids fluttered like a woman possessed. Her smile upped to blinding status, and both Ana and I simultaneously huffed.

"Who's she trying to impress?" Ana mumbled.

"Surely not Shelby." I giggled.

"How can I help you?" the officer purred to Charlie.

"Hi. I was hoping to have a chat with Officer Shelby."

"He's out the back. I'm Officer Madison Keating. Maybe I can assist you?"

"Pleased to meet you, Madison. I'm Charlie O'Sullivan. I've never seen you around here before."

"It's my second day." She beamed. "This is my first posting."

"Then welcome to Dandelion Ponds."

"Charlie O'Sullivan. That name sounds familiar." A faint line deepened between her perfect brows, and she bit on a pen as I watched the cogs turning in her brain. "Hmmm, how do I know that already?"

"Charlie! What are you doing here?" Trent Shelby shuffled into the room, a steaming mug in his hand.

"Looking for you. I was hoping to chat about Logan."

"I'm not happy sharing case information with a potential suspect if that's what you're after." Shelby straightened his shoulders as he placed the cup on the counter. Officer Keating's eyes widened as her lips formed an O. The penny had obviously dropped.

"You're that Charlie O'Sullivan," she gushed, dropping her pen on to the floor.

Shelby rolled his eyes at her before turning his attention back to Charlie.

"Come on. You don't seriously think I did it, do you?" Charlie replied.

"Your history with Logan doesn't work in your favor. You were at the hospital at the time of death, and you admitted to arguing with him only minutes before his body was found. What do you think?"

Charlie leaned back on his heels and studied Shelby. Officer Keating ignored the pen rolling across the vinyl floor and silently watched on as the clock ticked off the seconds.

"I think you know I'm innocent," Charlie finished.

Shelby deflated. "Yes, well that doesn't hold much weight, does it? I need proof. As it stands it's not looking good for you, Charlie."

"You want proof then I'll get it for you. Just give me some information to help me find it."

"I'm sorry, Charlie, but I can't do that. Now if you'll excuse me, I need to get some work done." Shelby subtly nodded toward Keating. He then cleared his throat and addressed her. "Officer Keating, we need to get that mail to the post office before this snowstorm gets any worse."

"Oh, of course," she replied, hurriedly grabbing a stack of envelopes. "I'll do that right away."

Pushing her arms into her jacket, she wrapped her scarf around her neck then donned her police cap and scurried from the room, unaware of the three envelopes she dropped as she skidded on the pen.

As the station door closed behind her, Shelby let out a breath. "She means well, but it seems she's a bit of a klutz."

Charlie bent to pick up the dropped mail and handed it to Shelby.

"I'm not saying I can help you, but what is it you need?" Shelby asked, tapping the envelopes on the countertop.

"Do you have copies of the CCTV footage from the hospital at the time of Logan's murder?"

Shelby paled. "Why do you ask that?"

"I'm hoping it shows who the real killer is."

"Things are never that easy."

"How so?"

Shelby dropped the mail and scrubbed his face with his palms.

"Look, Charlie, I can't show it to you."

"Come on! We both know I'm not guilty, and I think that footage proves it."

"It's not that."

"Care to elaborate?" Charlie pushed.

Shelby leaned his elbows on the counter and leaned into Charlie's space. "There's something bad going on in this town, and it's not just Logan's murder."

I shuddered "...something wicked this way comes," I whispered, as Shakespeare's words jumped to mind.

Charlie's eyes narrowed as he glanced my way before he

addressed Shelby. "I agree with you. And it all started with Daisy's attack."

"I believe it started long before then, but it does seem her attack was a big part of it all."

"And you think it's related to Logan's murder also?"

"I'm not sure. All I know is every time we get some evidence to prove what's happening, that evidence is corrupted or goes missing."

Charlie raised an eyebrow.

"The copies of the digital files we took from the hospital CCTV footage have been destroyed."

"You're kidding? How?"

"Apparently Officer Keating just got really nervous and spilt her coffee on the keyboard and when she tried to mop it up, she accidently deleted the files from the computer."

"What made her so nervous?"

"Liam Davenport smiled at her across the counter." Shelby moaned.

"In that case," I interrupted. "I don't blame her for being distracted. Liam is movie star good-looking and has the charm to go with it."

The corner of Charlie's lips tilted up.

"You couldn't get another copy of the file?" Charlie pushed.

"Yeah. We've requested the hospital send it through asap, but they're having technical difficulties at the moment." Fatigue burned in the dark rings beneath his eyes.

"You mean they've been erased too."

Shelby dropped his hands and stared at Charlie. "How do you know that?"

Charlie shrugged. "Lucky guess."

A muscle ticked below Shelby's eyes. "I'm sure the city detectives will be able to piece this mess together when they get here."

"When will that be?" Charlie asked.

"The snowstorm's cut the road to the city, but they should get through tomorrow."

"You don't look overly happy about that."

Shelby shook his head. "I just hope the hospital sorts the mess out and sends us the new copies of the files before they get here."

"And that the footage in the files shows who the killer really is," Charlie finished.

"Exactly."

"But you think there's something bigger happening?"

"I do. First, we had Daisy's attack, her co-worker is murdered, then her neighbor, and now her fiancé. I've written countless reports where the perp is adamant they committed crimes while sleep walking, and evidence keeps going missing or gets destroyed. You tell me it's not all connected." Shelby threw his hands in the air, his frustration evident. "What do you think Daisy knows that could help me piece this together?"

"I didn't know anything," I added. "Everything I'm learning has been since my coma."

Charlie turned his gaze to me as his jaw clenched. After a beat he said, "I heard Mike is having a few issues with some not so nice people."

Shelby jerked his head back. "What makes you say that?"

"Apparently someone is threatening him for money."

"Well, he hasn't reported anything to me. Regardless, what does that have to do with Logan's murder?"

"Did you know Logan resigned?"

"Yeah, but Mike wouldn't have killed him over that."

Charlie chewed the inside of his cheek as he watched Shelby. "Yeah, I agree," he breathed. "But did you look into the sale of Logan's office building?"

"Yep, nothing untoward about it. Logan was deeply in debt, and Amethyst Alexander had the money he needed."

"It's just…after you left there this morning, we saw a woman hiding in the shadows listening in on our conversation. When we saw her, she ran."

"We? I thought you were alone when I left you."

It was Charlie's turn to groan. "You wouldn't believe me even if I told you,"

"Try me."

"Maybe another day. When we both have a beer in our hands." Charlie grinned. "Trust me. You'll need it."

Shelby didn't look convinced. "Who was this woman you saw?"

"No idea. It was just odd she was watching from afar."

"That's not helpful."

"It's the best I can do at the moment."

Shelby's chest puffed before sharply deflating. "I'll do another drive-by and take a closer look, but I can't see what that building has to do with Logan's death. Amethyst Alexander got what she wanted when she paid it out, so she has no motive to hurt Logan."

"Was there another bidder?" Charlie asked, his look pointed to Logan.

Shelby obviously thought the question was for him. "I have no idea, but I'll ask around. Who knows? It may lead to something."

"Amethyst was the only one who knew the financial trouble I was in," added Logan.

"It still won't hurt for Shelby to do some digging," I finished.

After bidding bye to Shelby, we all followed Charlie back to his car.

His breath hung in the air as he pulled his coat close around his body, his hand shivering as he beeped the vehicle unlocked.

"Well, that was a bust. Definitely didn't tell us who the killer was." I moved to get into the back seat, but Ana pushed me aside.

"You know, I know a guy," she added as she moved into the back alongside Logan. "A dead tech guy. He once told me it's extremely difficult to completely erase files from a computer.

Even if the hospital is having technical difficulties, I'd bet the information we need is still on the police computers. We just have to find a way to access it."

"Great," I added. "That's easier said than done. I mean, it's not like any of us are computer geniuses."

Ana rolled her eyes. "I was going to suggest I ask him for help."

"Do it," Charlie agreed. "If we can learn who and what was on that footage, it might just end this for me." I got the impression he would be happy once Logan had passed to the other side.

Ana bobbed her head as she gave Charlie a megawatt smile, looking overly eager to please. I made a mental note to ask him about it later.

"But even if it is still there, and even if this computer genius knows how to access it, how do we do that?" I asked, as I slid onto the passenger seat next to Charlie. I momentarily wondered what Ana was up to as she never usually gave up that seat quite so easily. "He's dead, and it's not like any of us has actual hands."

"I do," Charlie said, wiggling his fingers.

"What are you suggesting?"

"If you can find someone who knows his way around a computer, and he can tell me exactly what I need to do, then I'll do it."

"But that would mean breaking into a police station!" My veins turned icy as I considered how much trouble Charlie was already facing.

"Not if I get Shelby onboard it won't." Charlie grinned.

"You think he'll believe you?"

"I know Shelby would like to get those files back before he's made to look stupid in front of the detectives. I also know he's motivated to solve what's really going on in this town."

"I guess you could always tell him you're the computer genius who knows his way around."

"Shelby's not that stupid," Logan scoffed.

Charlie hit him with a death glare.

"Look let's find the tech guy and then cross that bridge when we come to it," Charlie suggested.

"I'm on it," Ana declared. "It might take me a while to find him, but I'll get the job done." A small pop sounded, and she disappeared.

8

The frosted glass of the Victorian greenhouse reflected the eerie shadows the flickering candles created. Fog hung in tendrils close to the roof, and the starless sky threatened a cold night ahead.

Amethyst Alexander lovingly tended to the snake plant that twisted upward mingling with the lavender and peace lily. She snipped a few dead leaves from the deadly nightshade climbing the trellis and inhaled deeply as she moved to the powerful sleep-inducing valerian. Her sigh was deep and blissful.

"Not long now, my beauties," she cooed to the plants.

A hooded figure stood behind her, his breath ragged and laced with fear.

I pushed myself closer into the branches of the tall fir. Despite the fact I knew I was in someone's dream, I didn't want to be spotted.

Amethyst clipped a flower and spun toward the man, holding it close to his face. "You know what you have to do," she said to him, her voice hard, her dark eyes steely.

"Amethyst, I...I can't. Please." He stepped backwards as he raised his hands in surrender.

A woman moved from behind the potted laburnum, her face hidden in the shadows as she clung to the edges of the room.

"You know better than that," Amethyst warned. "The deal was I save your life, and you help us."

"But I...I can't do what you need. Please, please don't make me do it."

"Listen to me!" Amethyst snarled, her hands outstretched as she muttered under her breath. The vines swiftly grew, slithering their way toward the man and wrapping themselves around his ankle. "I have one chance to get what I need, and I can't have Daisy in my way. She's the only thing that can stop me."

"Then why don't you kill her yourself?" he asked, attempting to free his new binds.

Amethyst snapped her head up as if she'd been slapped. "You know I can't touch her. Her damn father put that stupid protection on her. No one in the Alexander lineage can harm her."

"Otherwise, we would have done it by now," the other woman, still hidden, added.

"Now," Amethyst placed a taloned fingernail on his chest, "New Year's Eve is approaching, and it's the only chance I will get in my lifetime. But Daisy needs to be gone before then. Do you understand?"

The man nodded slowly.

"Good. Now go and kill her."

The shadowed woman giggled as Amethyst pushed something into his pocket. He then bowed his head and turned to exit the greenhouse.

It was as he passed my hiding spot behind the trellis of English ivy that he looked up, and Logan's emerald-green eyes stared back at me.

I sat up, my own breath fast and uneven as my heart raced.

Early morning light snuck through a gap in the velvet curtains, the dawn of the last day of the year upon us. I turned to the man lying alongside me, snoring quietly, lost to the delicious depths of sleep, unaware of it all. I envied him.

"Charlie! Charlie, wake up. I need to talk to you."

Alfie stuck his snout from beneath the blankets, nose twitching as he looked up at me.

"Can you please wake Charlie up," I begged him.

Alfie stretched his legs out in front of him, lifting his butt in the air. After shaking himself off he then thankfully moved to Charlie and proceeded to lick his chin. Charlie absently swatted him away, but Alfie was nothing if not persistent.

"Cut it out," Charlie mumbled, as he pulled the blanket over his head.

I hurriedly ran around to face him. "Charlie! I need to talk to you!"

Throwing the blankets back, he fluttered his eyelashes, his eyes bleary and unfocused.

"I think I was in Logan's dream. I need to tell you what I learned."

"Daisy?" Charlie rubbed his eyes with his fists, rolling onto his back before sitting up against the pillow. "What are you talking about?"

"I slipped into someone's dream. I think it was Logan's, but I'm not sure."

"Does he still dream now that he's dead?"

"Ummm, I have no idea. But who else's dream would I be in?" I shook my head, my thoughts rapidly jumbling. "It did feel like there was someone standing behind me. I have no idea who it was though. Maybe I should have turned around and taken a look? But honestly it felt like I'd been invited into this dream. You know, like whoever's dream it was wanted me there, which is why I thought of Logan."

A small groan escaped Charlie's lips. "Daisy, there's obviously a point to this. Can you tell me what it is so I can go back to sleep? Please."

"Oh. Sorry. Amethyst Alexander gave Logan the order to kill me."

Charlie's eyes snapped open. That certainly got his attention.

"But Logan's dead," Charlie repeated, sitting up. "So, he's not threat to you now."

"I know, which is why the order must have been given a few days ago. Anyway, apparently something is happening on New Year's Eve, and I'm the only one who can stop Amethyst from achieving her goal."

"So, what you saw actually happened?"

"I think so."

"It sounds more like a memory."

"I agree, but I'm a night demon, which means I can enter people's dreams. I don't know if that stretches to their memories."

"It stuns me that you can have such power and yet know so little about it." Charlie sighed.

"Yeah, something I need to work on when I wake up. In the meantime, let's focus on what I just learned."

"If you actually learned anything."

It was my turn to sigh. "I need to ask Logan to verify it."

The sound of Charlie grinding his teeth grated on me. "If he was ordered to hurt you, then he's lucky he's dead already," he muttered.

Ignoring his not-so-veiled threat, I continued on. "The thing is, Charlie; New Year's Eve is today. And I'm still in a coma. How can I stop Amethyst without a body?"

"How do you stop her with one? And what are you preventing her from achieving? What's her plan?"

"Beats me!" I threw my hands in the air, anger bubbling in my chest. "But I can't sit by and do nothing."

"Okay, okay. Let's start by talking to Logan about what you saw. If it's true then…well, I don't know, but we'll figure it out. Together."

The anger was pushed aside by warmth borne in the knowledge Charlie was going to help me. That warmth travelled south as Charlie threw back the sheets and stepped out of bed, and I was rewarded with the glorious view of his half naked body. I made a mental note to thank Dorothy for keeping the heating up so high Charlie never felt the need to wear a shirt to bed.

Following him into the hall, I allowed him to do the shower/morning routine alone while I went in search of Logan.

It was always a surprise as to which spirits you would find hanging in Dorothy's kitchen in the mornings. She seemed to be a collector of lost souls. This morning Frank was there in all his glory chatting up Jason, the god-like chef who had passed to the afterlife while cooking crème brûlée.

He was now constantly looking for anyone living who would follow his instructions and cook up a feast. Today that was Dorothy.

"Sprinkle cayenne over those eggs while they're cooking," Jason instructed her, his incredible bicep flexing as he tensed. I took a moment to appreciate his beauty—his dark sparkling eyes, his long hair tied at the nape of his neck, and his beard trimmed to the perfect length. I released a blissful sigh before turning my attention to Dorothy.

To be honest she looked slightly worse for wear. Her hair was disheveled, her shirt was inside out, and her socks didn't match. Only as I noticed her sometimes boyfriend, Ken, sitting at the table looking just as tired, did I understand her state had nothing to do with Jason's teachings and more to do with her nighttime adventures.

"Morning," she trilled, ignoring Jason's pleas to turn the eggs over.

"Morning everyone," I replied as Frank leaned his elbows on the countertop, his dreamy eyes glued to Jason. "Where's Logan?"

"Ummm, last I saw him was last night," replied Dorothy. "He was on the couch talking to Ana."

Frank pulled his gaze from the cooking god and turned to me.

"Ana took him to a party in town. Said a change of scenery would do him good."

"But when are they coming back?" I asked, my stomach uneasy.

Frank shrugged. "I don't know. I'm not their keeper."

"Is everything okay?" Dorothy asked, finally flipping the eggs. Jason sagged against the counter, his hands running through his hair. I got the impression he wouldn't take up Dorothy's offer to cook for him in future.

"I need to talk to him urgently." I hurriedly brought everyone up to date with my dream.

"Frank, go and find Logan please," Dorothy commanded.

"What? Why me? Why is it always me?" he asked, his back straight and his perfect brows pulled into a V.

"Because you're the only spirit here who can transport." Her gaze flicked to Jason. "He doesn't count as I'm sure I'll burn these eggs without his supervision. And Daisy—well she hasn't perfected it just yet."

That was an understatement if ever I'd heard one.

Frank gave a long-suffering sigh but did as asked. He had just disappeared with a pop when Charlie wandered into the room, his hair wet from his shower.

Geez, Frank was going to be upset when he learned he missed it.

"Dorothy, you need to remove the bacon from the pan," begged Jason. "It's starting to resemble charred boards."

An alarming amount of smoke was coming from the frypan, but Dorothy didn't seem fazed. Instead, she pushed the bread into the toaster and grabbed two cups from an overhead cupboard before filling them with steaming black coffee.

If Jason had a body, I would have been worried he was going to pass out. Instead, he dropped his head into his hands, rocked on his heels, and started to hum some kind of mantra.

Ken flicked through the pages of the morning paper, ignoring it all.

"Can Ken see me?" I asked Dorothy, sitting alongside him.

"No."

"Then why doesn't he question you talking to yourself?"

"He's accepted her as crazy but loves her anyway," added Charlie, sitting opposite me.

Ken noticed Charlie and dropped the paper to say good morning.

"Hope we didn't keep you awake last night." He chuckled as he winked a hooded lid at Dorothy and a swath of grey hair fell over his eye.

"Not at all. Those ear plugs Mom gave me worked a treat."

"Can you get me some?" I begged. "Because I heard things that made me want to wash my ears out with acid."

Dorothy threw her head back and laughed. Jason groaned and shuffled toward the couch.

"Mom, you really should take that food off the heat before the neighbors call the fire department."

Dorothy turned to the pan as if noticing it for the first time. Thankfully, she removed it from the heat and flipped its contents onto a plate. It was as the toaster popped that a loud knock rattled the front door, making us all jump.

"Oh dear. Who could that be at this time of the morning?" Dorothy muttered, wiping her hands on a towel before padding into the hall.

We all sat silent, as Dorothy greeted whoever was at the door.

"Goodness, what is so urgent it can't wait until after breakfast?" she asked, as footsteps echoed toward us.

"I'm sorry for the intrusion." Officer Trent Shelby's voice followed. "I really am, but the powers that be…well I'm sure you understand what they're like."

Dorothy appeared around the corner, her lips pulled into a tight line, Shelby hot on her heels. He fiddled with the brim of his hat, snowflakes dusting his shoulders. As he connected eyes with Charlie, heat flushed his cheeks.

"Good morning," he said, nodding his head toward Ken. "Sorry to interrupt your…" His gaze landed on the charred bacon and eggs. "Breakfast?"

"Would you like to join us? I'm sure there's plenty for everyone," Dorothy added.

"Oh no! No, I don't want to intrude. Plus, I'm here on official business."

Charlie's back straightened, and his eyes hardened.

"I'm sorry, Charlie," continued Shelby. "But I'm here to ask you to accompany me to the station."

"What for?" he asked.

"The city detectives got through the storm last night and have more questions for you in regard to the murder of Logan Cutter."

"I've told you everything I know."

"Yes, well the hospital techs have informed us any CCTV footage of Logan's murder has been erased, and we have a witness who can place you near the security room around the time the files were tampered with."

Charlie's jaw clenched. "I can explain that."

"I really hope you can."

A plainclothes detective stood with his back to the wall, his lips pulled into a thin, tight line. His hairline was a distant memory, now compensated with the long salt-and-pepper beard bypassing his top shirt button. A second, younger detective sat opposite Charlie, the cold steel table separating them. His piercing blue eyes, manscaped stubble, and trendy haircut were very Zac Efron-ish, but that was the only part of him reminding me of the good-looking actor. His arrogance grated on my nerves as he scrambled to keep control of the interrogation.

Shelby waited by the door; his eyes narrowed. I would have liked to ask him if he had gas but decided his pain was being caused by the questions the detective was throwing at Charlie.

"So where were you at the time of the murder?" he asked.

As Ana stood protectively alongside him, Charlie sat ramrod straight, his jaw flexing, a vein in his temple throbbing. I leaned against the far wall and anxiously tapped my foot against the cushion of air beneath me.

"Detective Moody, I've told you three times already, I was in the bathroom."

The detective flipped through the paper strewn across the table. Lifting what looked like his scribbled notes, he said, "Previously you stated that you were walking to your car."

Ana scoffed and rolled her eyes.

Charlie exhaled loudly. "I'm sorry. I don't know the exact time of death so it's hard to pinpoint where I was."

"According to the coroner's preliminary report that was at eleven thirty-three a.m."

Charlie nodded.

"So where were you, Mr. O'Sullivan?"

"I have no idea where I was at that precise time. But as I've already explained, I left the ward and went to the bathroom where I splashed water on my face. Then I made my way to the car park."

"Did you stop along the way?"

"No."

"So, you didn't stop to collect a hospital scalpel?"

"I wouldn't even know where to begin to look for one of those."

"It's a hospital. I'd imagine they're everywhere."

"Is this guy for real?" Ana muttered.

"Then you know far more than I do," Charlie replied, before taking a deep breath.

"You seriously expect me to believe you don't know where you would find a scalpel in a hospital?"

"I'd guess maybe the operating theater, but I definitely did not go there. Nor did I ask the nurses for one or find any along my way."

"Do you own one?"

Charlie's mouth dropped open as his brow shot north. "No. I do not own a scalpel, but I'm guessing a scalpel was the murder weapon, then."

Moody ignored the question and made a few notes, the sound of a pencil scratching the paper the only thing competing with the ticking of the clock.

The older detective stepped forward, slamming his hands on the table. Lucky I had no physical body as I may have just peed my pants.

"Mr. O'Sullivan, you have a history with the deceased, do you not?" he demanded.

"If you mean we didn't get along then yes, we had a history."

"Our investigation has uncovered you were having an affair with his fiancée."

Charlie froze.

"Do you deny it?" The detective pushed.

"Yes, I deny it! I didn't even know Daisy before she fell into her coma."

"Then how do you explain your involvement with her now?"

Heat raced up Charlie's neck, a bead of sweat forming on his brow. Ana turned to me and scowled.

"We're friends," Charlie explained.

"Have habit out of befriending women in comas, do you? What's your motivation? To take advantage of them?"

"What exactly do you mean by that?" Charlie spat.

"We spoke to the hospital, and it seems that you're a regular visitor of Miss Montgomery. If you had never met her prior to her comatose state, then why were you there?"

Oh geez. Charlie seemed at a loss for words.

"Tell him we knew each other online, but we'd never met in person," I offered.

"Daisy and I had only ever corresponded online," Charlie lied.

"And you came to town with the intention of stealing her from her fiancé," Detective Moody pushed.

"No. I came to town to be closer to my mom."

"But when you saw Daisy Montgomery, you decided you needed to be with her," Moody continued.

"How would that work? Daisy's in a coma."

"According to the doctor she has a good chance of waking soon."

"And?"

"And I put it to you that you wanted to get rid of Logan Cutter so when Daisy woke you could console her, and thereby gain a place in her heart."

Charlie shook his head, his nostrils flared.

"Do you deny you are in love with Daisy Montgomery?"

Oh boy.

Charlie gulped, Ana looked like she wanted to faint, and I held my breath.

"I'll take your silence for a yes," the older detective added.

"What's your point in all of this?" Charlie asked.

"I think you killed Logan Cutter. You had the opportunity, and I can prove you were at the hospital guard's room, removing all evidence of the crime."

"I never removed anything."

"We'll see."

Detective Moody fidgeted in his seat as he side-eyed his older colleague.

A quiet knock sounded on the door behind Shelby. He silently opened it, and Officer Keating whispered something in his ear. Shelby paled as his gaze fell to Charlie before he quietly excused himself from the room.

A chill ran up my spine, and I took the opportunity to exit the room while the door was ajar. I didn't like leaving Charlie, but Ana had her eyes narrowed at the two detectives, and I figured as soon as she could learn how to give them the pox, she'd be cursing them to eternity.

"What do you mean, there's another murder?" Shelby growled, taking Keating's elbow and guiding her away from the closing door.

"We just had a call that a body has been found in a dumpster near Starlight Pond."

"Any more information than that?"

"Only that it's a young male dressed in a hospital security guard uniform. I made a few preliminary calls to the hospital, and it seems all guards are accounted for alive and well."

Shelby exhaled loudly. "Then we'd better get out there quick."

Keating nodded, her eyes darting back to the interrogation room. Shelby's gaze followed hers.

He groaned. "Don't worry, I'll tell the detectives. Be prepared though. They're going to want to accompany us to the scene."

Keating bit her lip, blinking rapidly. "And I thought this was going to be a good day."

9

Charlie led the way into the freezing air, his footsteps embedded in the new snowfall.

"We need to get to Starlight Pond and see what's going on," I pushed, hurrying to keep up with him as we made our way to the car. Once the detectives had heard the news about the body, they'd herded Charlie out the door demanding he be available whenever they needed him again.

"No way am I going anywhere near the crime scene. I'm staying as far from there as I can," he replied, his intent evident in his steps. "If this is connected to Logan's death, then I'm sure those detectives will somehow pin it on me."

"But aren't you curious as to who the victim is?"

"Not in the least."

"It's odd, right? A man dressed as a security guard is found dead."

"What are you suggesting?"

"That a fake guard broke into the security room at the hospital under instructions from a woman we saw running from the office building. We followed him to the hospital where he disappeared, and now he turns up dead."

"You don't know for sure it's the same guy," Charlie reminded me.

"Even I think that's odd," added Ana. "And I try quite hard not to agree with Daisy."

Charlie looked between the two of us, his gaze stopping on me. "You want me to drive to Starlight Pond and watch what the police are up to, in order to learn about the victim."

I nodded.

"And if you're right and this guy is connected to Logan's murder, then is it a good idea that I'm seen watching?"

"Well, I never thought of it like that," I mumbled, my chest deflating.

Charlie stopped walking as he stared at the horizon. "You're probably onto something though, Daisy."

"Really?" Excitement bubbled in my chest.

"Ahuh. I just don't think I should go." He spun a mischievous grin toward Ana. "But that doesn't mean you can't."

She balked. "What? Why me?"

"Because you can get there quickly, get the information without anyone even knowing you're there, and you agree it's a good idea."

"Why can't she go instead?" Ana hit me with a glare.

"Because I can't do the pop thing and disappear like you can."

Charlie beamed at her. "Come on. You want to prove my innocence, right? If Daisy is correct and this guy is the fake guard we saw at the hospital, it would be in my interest to find out who he was. Then maybe we can learn who he worked for and see if any of this is connected to Amethyst Alexander's plot. Whatever that may be."

Ana pouted.

"What else did you have planned for tonight?" I asked her.

Her pout turned to a scowl. "That's none of your business."

"I'd really appreciate it, Ana," Charlie added as his smile turned soft and intimate.

Her frown instantly melted. Not that I blamed her. His smile had the ability to thaw glaciers.

"Fine. I'll go and hang around those awful men while they fuss over another dead body and see what I can learn."

"Thank you."

She hit me with a death stare before disappearing in a flourish of popping noises.

"She was showing off, right?" I asked Charlie as he stepped off the footpath and toward his car.

"She always was dramatic." He pulled his car keys from his pocket and winked. I struggled to keep my knees from buckling as I placed my hand on my heart and took a few calming breaths, willing the effect Charlie had on me to slow. I suddenly wished I could feel the cool air as my soul was heating like a furnace. Taking a moment before I followed him to the car, I calmed my hormones by basking in the dreariness surrounding us.

My gaze fell to a woman stepping from the vehicle alongside Charlie's Mustang. I gasped. "Oh, my goodness! It's Lilli!"

"Where?" Charlie asked, stopping dead in his tracks.

"Walking toward you!"

Anger churned in my stomach as my blood boiled remembering every bad thing she had done.

Her long, unbuttoned trench coat billowed behind her as her knee-high boots kicked the snow aside. She looked up, and her eyes locked onto Charlie.

"What are you doing here?" he asked her.

"I could ask you the same question," she snarled, flicking her long auburn ponytail over her shoulder

"She did it! I bet she was the one who killed Logan!" I declared stepping between her and Charlie.

She shivered and pulled the coat tight around her willowy frame.

Charlie ignored me and continued to stare at Lilli as he absently rubbed the wound her bullet had given him. "You know you're in violation of the restraining order I have on you. You're not allowed within three hundred feet of me."

"Then I suggest you get out of my way." Her gaze was withering.

"You didn't answer my question. What are you doing here?"

"It's none of your business, but if you must know my bail condition states I have to sign in daily."

"But you were in the city."

"Yes, well, family matters brought me home."

I stepped into her space. This close I could see the dark rings hidden beneath her make-up, strain showing in the deep creases at the corners of her eyes. Her usually bright grey eyes were dull, and she looked more tired than I had ever seen her.

I wasn't one to be vindictive, but what she had done to those I loved was unforgiveable, and I was glad she wasn't enjoying her current position.

She hugged her arms over her body and stepped around Charlie. "Now if you'll get out of my way, I might just be able to stick to the restraining order."

He allowed her to pass as I attempted to grab his arm.

"She did it!" I yelled at him. "I know she did."

He released a slow breath as our eyes connected, but he waited until we were in the car before he responded.

"Why would Lilli kill Logan?" Charlie turned toward me, his gaze sincere.

"It has to be connected to the office building! She must have had a reason for wanting him to purchase it and keep her involvement a secret. What if he threatened to tell the town about it all?"

Charlie chewed his lip as he started the car. "I don't know Daisy. That doesn't sound like a good enough reason to kill someone."

"She had motive." I pushed, my theory gaining strength with

every syllable. "Her being in town proves she had opportunity. What more do you want?"

"Proof."

"You need to talk to Shelby about it."

"Why?"

"He knows you're innocent."

Charlie blew out a breath.

"If you can at least get him to look into it, it might just get those detectives off your back," I added.

"We'd need to give him some proof of why we think Lilli is the killer."

"Then let's get him proof! Plus, we might learn what importance it all holds to Amethyst. Even if I don't wake in time, I've been wondering if I can use my dreams to stop whatever plot she has planned for tonight."

I could see from the glint in Charlie's eye I was winning my case. I grinned and pushed on. "Now come on, what are we waiting for?"

"Directions. I have no idea where to go next."

I bit my lip, running through possibilities of what happened that night. "Let's go home and see if Logan knows more than he thinks."

"Okay. But I'm going to grab some lunch on the way. I'm starving."

"What are you having to eat?" I asked.

"I was going to stop at the bakery and get a pie and wash it down with a cola." Charlie rubbed his stomach before putting the car in gear and steering it out of the parking lot.

I groaned. When I woke up food was the first thing I was asking for.

As Charlie licked his lips, I hurriedly reassessed my priorities.

Dorothy put the last pot in the dishwasher and leaned her hip against the counter as she wiped her hands on her floral apron. Her brows knitted as she considered Charlie's question. "Logan's not here. When you were taken for questioning Ana wanted to be with you, so Frank took Logan out to get his mind off things."

"Can you call Frank?" Charlie asked as Alfie jumped into his lap, turned three concentric circles, and snuggled in for a nap.

I sat heavily on the nearest chair and sighed.

Dorothy grinned. "He'll come quicker if you call."

"I feel stupid calling for a ghost."

"When are you ever going to accept you have the gift?" Dorothy asked, moving to sit at the table alongside him.

"I do not have any kind of gift."

Dorothy nodded to Alfie.

"He's not fussy. He'll sit in anyone's lap," Charlie explained.

"No, he won't," I interjected. "He's actually quite picky."

"He sits with Elsie all the time."

"Ahuh. She's a good person. He only likes good people."

Charlie grinned. "I'm not going to win this argument, am I?"

Both Dorothy and I shook our heads.

"So, tell me everything that happened at the station," Dorothy pushed. "I need to know if I'm cursing anyone."

I gave a hollow laugh. "Get your spell book ready. Those detectives were awful."

Charlie brought her up to date with their interrogation. Once he'd finished, she stood and exited the room, muttering something about hair loss and facial warts.

"Have your dog." Charlie placed Alfie on the chair where I was sitting and pushed away from the table. "I need a drink."

Alfie fell through my aura and landed on the wooden seat. I couldn't feel him in the same way I could Charlie, but my soul felt happy when he was close. As Alfie settled and closed his eyes, I figured he sensed the same thing.

Charlie had just finished pouring himself a bourbon when Dorothy re-entered the room.

"I found it!" she declared. *"The Enormously Large Book of Curses.* I haven't used it in a long time, but I knew I still had it somewhere." She dropped a thick, leather-bound book onto the table, and we all jumped at the thump it made.

Charlie eyed the book. "Mom, you're not seriously going to curse them, are you?"

"You can bet your last dollar I am." She licked her finger before flipping the dusty old pages, her glasses perched on the end of her nose. "Oh, this is the one. Now what do I need? Black candle. Hemp. Oh, I need some of their hair." She lifted her eyes to Charlie. "Can you get me some please?"

"You want me to get hair from the two detectives who want to arrest me for murder? How do you propose I do that? Walk up to them with scissors and just cut myself what you need?"

She rolled her eyes. "It only needs to be a single strand. I don't need a lock of it."

"Yeah? Well, one of them is bald already," Charlie replied before emptying his second glass of alcohol.

"What are you cursing them with?" I asked, reading over her shoulder. I grimaced. "Three Nights of Hell sounds serious."

"Pfmt. It's nothing more than a few sores. But it may make them think twice next time they're so rude."

"Where will the sores erupt, exactly?"

Dorothy wiggled her eyebrows, and I giggled.

Charlie stuck his fingers in his ears and started to hum.

"Is there anything in that book that can help me wake up?" I asked, ever hopeful.

"I've been working on that one. I think I'm nearly there, but I have a few things to organize."

I sat up straight, a lightness in my soul pushing the heaviness away. I was about to question Dorothy about it more when a popping sound interrupted us, and Ana appeared in all her glory.

"Please don't ever ask me to oversee a dead body for you again," she pleaded as Charlie poured a third glass. "I realize I'm surrounded by dead people all the time, but to actually see the gore of how they died isn't something I enjoy."

"Who did they find?" I asked, not wanting her to explain the details.

"The kid I saw at hospital. His throat was cut and his body dumped. It was gruesome."

"That's too sad." My heart cracked for a guy I'd never known.

"That's the same way Logan died," Charlie added.

"A detail that didn't escape Shelby," Ana added.

"Do the detectives still think Charlie killed Logan?" I asked.

She nodded, and a weight settled in my belly.

"Great. Now we have two murders to solve."

"Shelby's not in agreement though. I heard him arguing with them about it. The coroner said the time of death was around ten last night. So, Charlie, you can expect more questions about your whereabouts."

"I was in bed."

"With only your family who can verify that. The police already think Dorothy is a biased witness," Ana said.

"I'm betting the woman who engaged the kid to do her bidding is the killer," I mused. "And that would mean it's the same person who killed Logan. And I'm also betting that's the same woman who was hiding in the shadows in the dream."

"But we still don't know who she is."

"It's Lilli!" I yelled, forcing my hands onto my hips. "Why aren't you all as convinced as I am?"

A loud pop followed by a flash made me squeal as Frank and Logan appeared in the room. Frank was beaming as he held Logan's hand, and Logan looked like he wanted to be sick.

"Did you see that?" Delight twinkled in Frank's eyes. "Sophia taught me how to do the flash thing."

"Impressive," I mumbled, side-eyeing Charlie and Dorothy.

"Do you ever get used to the dizzy feeling?" Logan asked as Frank released his hold.

"Yeah. It takes a few times, but it soon passes."

"Where have you two been?" Dorothy asked, ignoring me and closing the spell book with a wallop.

"I've been showing Logan how to scare Kitty." Frank guffawed. "I think I have a new career ahead of me. I'm going to be the one to demonstrate to the newbies how to get around. Show them the ropes, so to speak."

"What did you think of that, Logan?" Dorothy asked.

He shrugged. "It was better than sitting around here."

"There's nothing wrong with doing just that." Dorothy tutted as she picked up her crochet needles and wool.

"Sorry, I didn't mean to sound so…"

"Insulting?"

Logan grimaced and sat alongside me.

"We saw Lilli today," I said to him as he leaned his elbows on the table and placed his head in his hands. "She's out on bail and back in town. I think she was the one who killed you. She's gone on to kill again."

"We don't know that," Charlie warned.

Logan hurriedly dropped his hands as he emphatically shook his head. "No. Lilli didn't do it."

"How can you be so sure?" I flattened my lips as I dared him to argue.

"Because she would never hurt me."

"Huh. You sound pretty confident about that." I crossed my arms over my chest and glared at him.

Frank remained quiet, his head darting between Logan and me. Dorothy sat opposite Logan, her crochet needle moving at double speed.

"I *am* confident," Logan said. "Look, Lilli and I…well…she was in love with me."

My eyes shot open. "She's engaged to Mark!"

"That was because her mother wanted a union of their families. Didn't you know that?"

"No. I thought he was the love of her life."

"She played the part well."

"Obviously. But what's so special about his family that Amethyst wanted them united?"

"I'm not exactly sure, but I know they're growers in the south. What they grow I don't know."

"Hang on. I met his mother at their engagement party. Isn't she a naturopath?" I searched my memory for the half-hour conversation I had with her.

"Yes, but they grow their own product. You've seen it at Lilli's. It's the stuff growing in the pot on the kitchen counter. Lilli told me it enhances healing or something like that."

I shook my head to clear my thoughts. "We're getting off track. Why do you think Lilli was in love with you?"

"Because she once told me so."

"And you never thought to mention this to me?"

"It's not the easiest thing to tell your fiancée."

Tell me about it.

"And how did you feel about her?" I asked, not sure if I wanted the truth or not.

"Daisy, I love you, no one else, and I told her that."

My throat thickened as guilt for my feelings for Charlie twisted my stomach.

"When I found out what she did, I broke all ties with her. I haven't seen her since she was arrested."

"But you accepted money from her mom to pay out the building," Charlie snarled.

Logan stood and paced the room. "Amethyst wanted that building for her own reasons. I have no idea what that reason is, but she was adamant."

"Why did Lilli want it to begin with?" I asked.

Logan shrugged. "She told me she wanted me to have

everything I'd ever desired, and if her financial backing me got me that, then she was always there to help."

I bit my lip as my recent dream overrode all memories, demanding attention. "Logan, I saw you with Amethyst in a dream."

"What are you talking about?" Logan asked slowly, his expression guarded.

I hurriedly brought him up to speed. By the time I'd finished his head hung so low his forehead was almost lying on the table.

"What did Amethyst give you?" Anger boiled and pushed all my guilt aside.

"Daisy…I need to explain."

"What did she give you?" I asked.

"It was some kind of plant," he mumbled, rubbing his face.

"Do you still have it?"

"Yeah. She said I was to leave it under your pillow at the hospital."

"Amethyst demanded that?" Charlie asked.

Logan shrugged. "No. There was someone else in the room, but I never saw her face. That was the first time I'd encountered her, and she stayed hidden in the shadows."

"Do you still have the plant?" Dorothy asked, as her needle clanged on to the tabletop.

Logan nodded, then pushed his hands into his pockets and retrieved a long, fernlike seedling.

"I've seen that before," I said, screwing my nose up in concentration.

"What is it?" Charlie leaned close.

Dorothy copied him, but as Logan was a spirit, it seemed whatever he once had in his pocket was also no longer physical.

"I think that's wolfsbane," announced Dorothy. "I've read about the effects it can have. Hang on, I'll go and find the book." She stood and scurried from the room, as I searched my memory for where I'd seen it recently.

"Maybe you've used it in a bouquet," suggested Charlie.

"No. It was growing wild. I just can't pinpoint where that was."

"Why is it important?"

"Because if Logan could use it against me, then maybe I can do the same thing."

Charlie opened his mouth to respond, as Dorothy hurried back toward us, an open book in her arms, the title inscribed on the spine. *The Encyclopedia of the World's Deadliest Plants.*

"Here it is!" she announced. "This is basically the idiot's guide to poisonous plants in the 1800s and has come in handy on more occasions than I care to list. Now, there used to be a poisonous garden in Dandelion Ponds. Apparently, some rich European princess moved here in the early 1700s. She built a home with her husband and decided it would be fun to plant a garden full of poisonous plants."

"The Lethal Garden," I whispered.

"Yeah. You've heard about it?"

"I've dreamt about it. It's where the first night demon performed a ceremony under a lunar eclipse that gave her the power she needed to rule."

"How's that connected to Amethyst giving a plant to Logan?" Ana asked.

"I don't know exactly, but Amethyst certainly draws her power from plants," I said, "and that's probably the reason her greenhouse is full of those that can cause you harm."

"Wolfsbane certainly fits that description." Dorothy read from the yellowed pages. "It contains an alkaloid called aconitine. It disables nerves, lowers blood pressure, and can stop the heart when ingested."

"Logan, in the dream—'

"Memory," interrupted Charlie.

"Whatever. Anyway, Logan, Amethyst gave you the instruction to kill me." The anger once again churned.

Logan lowered his gaze. "I would never harm you, Daisy. Never!"

I crossed my arms over my chest. Did I believe him?

"So why did Amethyst ask *you* to do it?" I pressed.

He crumpled into the chair and hid his face behind his hands. "There're things you don't know about me," he said, quietly.

"Then bring me up to date," I snapped.

Logan lifted his unblinking gaze toward the ceiling as seconds ticked into minutes, leaving us all lost in the silence waiting for his next word.

"Lilli and I met a long time ago," he finally began, "before I moved to Dandelion Ponds." He rubbed his hands on his jeans, screwing his eyes shut tight. "Dad and I hadn't long lost Mom, and I was getting myself into trouble around the town we lived in. Dad thought it was a good idea for me to go to summer school. He wanted to get me out of the gang I was hanging with to meet some new friends. It was also an excuse for him to drink himself into oblivion without having to worry about me stealing from his liquor cabinet."

I nodded, knowing those early days had been hard for both Logan and his father.

"Lilli and I met at orientation, and we instantly struck up a friendship. Over the next few weeks, we became inseparable. We were both bored with the camp and the activities they thought we should be completing, and we tended to just take off and do our own thing. The leaders got sick of us eventually and called our parents. Of course, my father was drunk and didn't care one way or another what I did, but I'll never forget seeing Amethyst for the first time. She arrived at camp to talk to Lilli, and if I'm honest, she was terrifying. All long hair and flowing clothes billowing in her wake."

He shivered. "She and Lilli argued, and it ended with Lilli running away. I followed as she ran toward the forest around the lake's edge. What I didn't know at the time was another kid, Jose, who had a serious crush on Lilli was also following her. I found him leering at her from behind the trees. He was a sniveling little creep. I guess in hindsight I had some pent-up anger over my dad not even bothering to turn up to see what I was doing. Anyway, I grabbed Jose by the collar and dragged him out of his hiding place, and a fight broke out. Lilli tried to stop us, but teenage anger is real. Anyway, the fight ended when Jose hit me with a rock and I fell into the water. I woke with Lilli holding my head and crying as Amethyst was chanting and pushing leaves into my mouth."

"What had happened?" I asked.

"It seems Jose had knocked me out cold and when I fell in the water I was drowning. Lilli pulled me to safety, but I wasn't breathing. So, she ran and found her mother. Whatever Amethyst did for me brought me back from death."

I sucked in a sharp breath. "You died?"

Logan shrugged. "I don't know for sure, but from what Amethyst told me, yes."

"But there's no way to bring the dead back to life," Charlie said, his eyes darting from Logan to Dorothy.

"I've heard," started Dorothy, her voice quiet, "there's a small window after we die where we have the chance to return."

"Then why weren't *we* brought back to life?" Frank asked, speaking up for the first time as his eyelashes batted at an alarming rate.

"Because the help that's given has to be a certain kind of help," Dorothy finished.

"Like black magic, you mean," I added.

Dorothy nodded.

Logan coughed to clear his throat. "Lilli told me she begged her mother to help me. She felt responsible for what happened as I was defending her from Jose. It was only recently Amethyst informed me she only saved me because she had a plan for my future. Once I got home from camp, Dad changed. He drank heavier, withdrew even more until I barely knew him."

"Did you stay in touch with Lilli?" I asked.

Logan nodded and lowered his eyes.

"Why did neither of you ever tell me this?"

"Lilli asked me not to," he replied quietly.

"Was moving here part of Amethyst's plan for you?" I swallowed down the hurt that rose in my throat as even more of Logan's deceptions came to the surface.

Logan nodded. "Yeah. Over the years whenever Lilli and I hung out, Amethyst would remind me of what she had done. When Amethyst asked me to move to the Ponds, it was with the intention of getting to know you, Daisy."

"Why?" I cried. "I was already friends with Lilli, so if she needed information then she already had a way to get it."

Logan shook his head. "No. Lilli hated telling her mother anything and would avoid it the best she could."

"But you told Amethyst everything she wanted to know…" I whispered as I sat down hard on the nearest chair and held my hand over the mounting pressure in my chest.

"No! Well, at first yes. But I quickly realized what I felt for you was real. That changed everything, Daisy. You have to believe that."

"Why do I? Logan, you've done nothing but deceive me." I pinched my lips against the tremble that threatened tears.

"No! Well…yes. But it was so I could protect you."

"Why does Amethyst need someone else to do her bidding?" asked Charlie, cutting in.

"Because anyone from the Alexander lineage can't hurt me," I finished as Logan's gaze locked onto mine.

"Daisy, I told them I would never do it." His eyes filled with moisture as they pleaded with me to believe him. "You haven't been shown enough of the dreams. You haven't seen where I stood up against them."

"Did they listen?"

"No, but *I* had a plan. When you woke up from the coma, I was going to tell you what they were doing and get you to leave with me."

"That would put a target on your back," Frank squeaked.

"Maybe."

"What does Amethyst want from you, Daisy?" Charlie pushed. "What does she need you for?"

I shrugged and pulled my gaze away from Logan and the intensity burning in his eyes. "All I know is my dad passed his powers to me once he died. Maybe she's threatened by that?"

"But why now? Why not get Logan to kill you when you first met him?"

"There has to be a clue in the dream," Dorothy added.

"You said something is happening tonight, New Year's Eve." Questions flashed in Charlie's eyes.

I turned to Logan. "Did Amethyst ever tell you what that was?"

He shook his head. "She never told me anything I didn't need to know."

"None of this is proving who killed Logan," Ana reminded us.

"It was Lilli!" I shouted. "She's Amethyst's puppet—"

"You're wrong." Logan interrupted. "She would never hurt me, but I have wondered if…"

"If what?"

"Well, Lilli isn't an only child." Logan sat back and crossed his arms.

"I know. She has a brother."

"Yes, Lilli does have a brother, but her mother also has a daughter from a previous relationship," Logan explained.

I froze, my eyes wide as my eyebrows disappeared somewhere around my hairline.

"So, what happened to her?" Charlie asked.

"As far as I knew she lived in New York with her father." Logan shrugged.

"How did I never know this? Lilli and I told each other everything." I fell against the chair back, my shoulders sagging with the revelation.

"Not everything. She was only allowed to tell you what you needed to know."

My mouth dropped open. "You were my fiancé! You say you love me, yet you never thought to tell me any of this?" I thought I'd led a wonderful life, surrounded by friends who loved me. Boy, was I gullible to have fallen for that.

"I wanted to, Daisy, but Amethyst said if I ever whispered even a syllable to you then she would kill me." Logan slumped in his chair. "I wondered if the daughter was the other woman in the room the night Amethyst gave me the order to...you know."

"Murder me?" My tone was as flat as my mood.

Charlie stood and paced the room, his look dark as it locked onto Logan. "You're lucky you're already dead," he snarled.

"I was never going to do it! You have to believe that, Daisy. I just needed to keep my promise to Amethyst all while I was planning how to get you out of town. No one knew my plan..."

"Least of all me." I huffed.

"But if Amethyst got wind of it, then she could have had you killed for sure," Dorothy finished.

"How would she have gotten wind of it?" Logan asked.

"Dreams. She visited your dreams," I reminded him. "It's how she controls those in this town."

"She doesn't control everyone," Dorothy added.

"I know. But what if her plan is to overrule even the strongest of us?" Pieces of the puzzle began to fall into place as thoughts drifted over everything I'd learned since waking in the coma. The evil that

Shelby had spoken to Charlie about, the way kids were controlled to do things they wouldn't otherwise do. All the horrible events that had taken place in Dandelion Ponds made complete sense when falling into this new realization. A distant dream stirred. "It's what she wants. To become the most powerful night demon there is."

Silence echoed loudly as everyone stared back at me, their mouths agape.

Finally, Frank squeaked, "How do we prove it?"

I dropped my head into my hands and closed my eyes as voices filled the air around me. It appeared they all had a theory, but my thoughts whirred as they scrambled for first place, all wanting to be put in their rightful home.

Why was Logan at the hospital when he died? If Amethyst had ordered him killed, then why there? She had far better opportunities in the middle of the night when he was fast asleep. In fact, with her power she could have convinced him to do it himself!

"Logan," I interrupted Frank's musings on how the mysterious daughter had managed the deed.

Everyone turned their attention to me.

"The day you died…is that why you were at the hospital?" I asked, not really wanting the answer. "You were going to plant the wolfsbane, but Charlie was there instead?"

"No!"

"How can you be so sure? You say you don't remember what happened that day. Is the wolfsbane the key to Amethyst controlling me?"

Logan vigorously shook his head.

"Logan, you had it in your pocket," Charlie reminded him.

"I didn't visit the hospital to kill Daisy, nor to allow anyone else to do it! I'd die first."

I gasped.

"No, no, no, no." I put my hand in the halt position wanting to stop his words. "Please tell me that's not what happened? Tell me you weren't killed protecting me!"

Logan paled. Dorothy placed the book on the couch and moved to sit beside him.

"Is Daisy right?" she asked.

It took Logan a moment, his eyes lost in his thoughts. "I...I don't know. I honestly don't know who killed me or why. The last thing I remember is walking out of the hospital and toward the parking lot. I was hit by a smell and then there's nothing after that."

"I think the smell was the root of a plant named Mimosa pudica," Dorothy added. "When it's damaged it releases a cocktail of sulfur compounds. The smell was there to keep others away."

"But why?"

"So the murderer could do what they needed to do."

"But if this was premeditated, why there?" I asked. "Why not wait until Logan was near his car?"

"So, what do you think?" Dorothy asked me.

"I think it was a chance encounter. The killer saw their opportunity and took advantage of it."

"And they just carry this plant around in their pocket for times when they need to keep people away?"

I lifted my shoulders. "Who knows? When it comes to the Alexanders, anything is possible."

"You now think Amethyst killed Logan?" Charlie asked me.

"No. She's not the kind of person to do her own bidding."

"Then who do you think did it?"

"The elusive daughter."

"And who is that?"

I shrugged.

"You know what?" yelled Logan. "I don't care who killed me. It doesn't matter. I deserved what I got."

"No one deserves to be murdered," I added, despite the fact that I had momentarily considered it myself a minute ago. "But it matters that we learn who did it. Not only to give you peace and justice to whoever that was, but I believe it's connected to Amethyst's plan for tonight."

"Talk me through what you're thinking," Dorothy encouraged.

"It's the timing of it all. Why now? Several attempts have been made on my life recently. The dream showed me that I'm the threat to Amethyst and she needs me out of the picture. If I'm right and she wants to rule the town, then who's doing her bidding this time and what threat do I pose to her?"

Charlie clenched his jaw. "You're right. After the last attempt we thought you were safe. But all the time that Amethyst is around we need security on your hospital door. I'm going to call Shelby and ask if he can afford an officer to stand guard."

"You're wasting your time, Charlie. Amethyst has the power to control anyone. She'll influence the guard without hesitation."

"I have to try, Daisy. I can't leave you there unprotected." He gulped and fear danced in his eyes.

"I think we're better off tracking down who killed Logan. If we know who that is, maybe I can use my powers against them to learn exactly what she plans to do tonight and where."

Charlie held my gaze as a myriad of emotions travelled between us. Fear, sadness, anxiety, and desperation all mixed with longing and desire. Mine wasn't only a physical desire to hold him, but also for this to be behind us. For me to wake up and be able to live my life alongside him, free from fear.

Unspoken words danced on his lips, and I knew that the love he felt for me was very different from that Logan had. Charlie would never betray me or deceive me no matter the cost. I could trust him with my life.

He nodded before turning away. "Ana, did you ever track down your computer nerd friend?"

"He prefers to be known as a computer genius," she said. "And I've kind of tracked him down."

Charlie cocked an eyebrow as I allowed the beating inside my chest to settle, words tangling on my tongue.

"My friend Bentley told me he was at some gaming expo but should be back in town this evening."

"Great. How will you know when he's back?" Determination steeled on Charlie's lips. "Should you go and find him?"

Ana's hair ruffled as she blew out an exaggerated breath. "Fine. I'll go, but seriously, Charlie, we need a talk about how many errands I do for you."

"I thought you said your job was to be his guardian angel," I reminded her.

"I haven't checked the manual lately, but I'm pretty sure that dog's body doesn't come under the job description of guardian angel," she snapped.

"I've told you before you're free from your duties." Charlie released a long breath.

"Urgh! I'll be back as soon as I've found him." A loud pop sounded as she disappeared.

Charlie leaned back in his chair and ran his hands through his hair.

"I think I need a drink."

"You've just had three," Dorothy reminded him.

"Yeah, and the bottle is now empty. A beer at The Weed Killer sounds like a good idea."

Dorothy rolled her eyes. "It's only lunchtime."

"Then the bar should be full of the lunch crowd." Charlie continued as he scraped his chair backwards. "This town is full of gossips. I may just be able to learn who our latest murder victim was and what Amethyst needed to know."

10

Charlie pushed the door to The Weed Killer open, and laughter blasted out into the street as our friends and neighbors celebrated the season with their favorite beverages. Glasses tinkled and competed with the replay of an old basketball game being shown on the big television screen, and the room buzzed with excited chatter. Winter days were short and dark, and the residents of the Ponds didn't like to be outside longer than necessary. As Charlie elbowed his way through the crowd, I realized they didn't like to be at home either.

Not that I blamed them. Inside The Weed Killer was cozy, and on a cold day it was most welcoming. Overhead lighting hung from industrial beams. The walls and the ceiling were painted black, and the floor was scarred timber. Red brick lined the wall behind the bar where shelves held row after row of spirits, just asking to be consumed. Frosted beer taps took pride of place on the bar top, local craft beers at the ready, and the owner, Brayden, smiled at Charlie as he held an empty glass at the ready.

"The usual?" he asked, his shaggy blond man bun tied messily at his neck. Leather bracelets adorned his wrists, and his tan was sprayed on. Brayden had the relaxed surfer look perfected to a fine art.

Charlie responded with a smile and a nod. "Yeah, a Pond Scum please."

I grimaced and took a seat on the barstool alongside him.

"It tastes delicious," Charlie whispered from the side of his lips.

"I'll take your word for it."

We'd left Logan at home with Dorothy and Frank. He'd been upset after confessing the truth about Lilli, and we'd both decided it would be good to have a time out from each other for a while.

"How are you, Charlie?" Brayden interrupted my thoughts as he exchanged a full glass of beer for a few bills from Charlie.

"I've been better," Charlie responded honestly.

Brayden nodded. "I had a couple of city detectives in here this morning asking about a fight you had with Logan Cutter a week back. Sounded like they're building a case against you."

Charlie paled. "I didn't kill him."

"I know you didn't. Despite the bookies having you down as the favorite you're far too obvious. I watch enough TV to know it's never the obvious ones who are guilty." Brayden laughed.

Charlie's mouth dropped open. "They're taking bets on me?"

"Yeah, but don't worry. No one really believes you did it." Brayden pulled a cloth from his shoulder and wiped the bar as he smiled at Charlie.

"Who else is on the betting sheet?" Charlie asked.

"A few believe Logan's boss, Mike, was involved, but they're just making a story out of nothing if you ask me."

"Did Mike deserve that?"

"Not in my opinion. He was known to have a few arguments with Logan, but if that's the prerequisite to getting on the list, then half the town would be suspect."

"Logan fought with a lot of people?"

"Only when he drank too much." Brayden grinned. "Hey, Shelby!" he called, looking past Charlie to the man now inching his way closer. "What can I get you?"

Shelby looked strained. His skin was sallow, shadowy rings lined his eyes, and he absently flipped his cap between his fingers.

"Make it something strong," he ordered Brayden. "And keep them coming."

"Bad day?"

"The worse." He threw his cap on the bar, dropped onto a bar stool, and rubbed his eyes with his thumbs.

Charlie remained quiet as Brayden filled a shot glass with something from the top shelf.

"Hit me with one of those too, please," Charlie asked. "It's been that kind of day."

Shelby jolted before upending the glass to his lips. He then nodded toward Brayden to fill it back up. "You might as well leave the bottle there. I'm going to need it." He seemed to get lost in his thoughts as Charlie drummed his fingers on the bar top, biding his time before speaking again.

"I heard there was a second murder." Charlie downed the shot and placed his glass alongside Shelby's.

Shelby considered him for a moment before he exhaled loudly and refilled both glasses.

"I've been doing this job for a lot of years, and I've seen more than my fair share of death, but some just hit harder than others."

I gulped as pain burned bright in his eyes.

"Gruesome?"

We both knew the answer as Ana had informed us of those details.

Shelby downed a second shot and shivered as it went down. He hurriedly refilled it.

"I can accept a young life being taken in an accident. It's awful, but it happens. But to know there's a person out there who did something so horrific to someone so young breaks me."

"Who died?"

"You don't know?" Shelby fixed his gaze on Charlie for a moment, and I held my breath as all the sounds in the bar disappeared into the background.

"Why would I?"

"You weren't the one to kill him?" Shelby's eyes narrowed as he studied Charlie.

"I don't even know who *he* is."

The world momentarily stopped spinning as I waited for Shelby's response. "You know, Charlie, I have no reason to believe you."

"But you do anyway?"

Shelby lifted the bottle and poured the clear liquid into both glasses. Pushing Charlie's closer to him, he then lifted his own to his lips.

Only when both glasses were once again empty did Shelby speak again. "You know what I hate, Charlie? I hate men who come into my town and think they know more than I do about it."

"Moody and Ogilvy?" Charlie asked, referring to the city detectives.

"They throw their weight around and try to tell me I have no idea about anything happening in Dandelion Ponds. But you see, that's where they've made their mistake. I see things. I hear things. I *know* things." Shelby tapped his temple as he drew out the last few syllables. It appeared the alcohol was already having its desired effect.

"I believe you," replied Charlie, filling Shelby's glass for him this time. "Those detectives are obnoxious and rude."

"You should have seen how they treated Officer Keating. It was disrespectful and disgusting. Just because she's young and new to the job, it doesn't make her stupid." Hatred tightened his lips. "She may be clumsier than most, but she'll make a good police officer—one day," he added, accepting Charlie's offering.

"True, she didn't handle things well today, but seeing that young man's lifeless body was enough to make anyone sick."

Shelby drained the glass.

"Who was he?"

"It's confidential. Part of an ongoing case."

"Come on. We both know how fast gossip spreads around this town. Word's probably already out."

"Yeah, I did have to send Bixby packing. He was trying to get the scoop for the morning paper." Shelby shook his head. "But relatives need to be told before he can spread that kind of thing around."

"Have you told the family?"

"Yeah. That's what brought me here. I hate this part of the job. I mean, how do you tell the mother of a teenager her son has been murdered and you suspect he was somehow tangled up in an ongoing murder investigation."

"How so?" Charlie probed.

Shelby sighed. "It appears when a computer genius is needed to erase hospital records then the high school is the place to recruit."

"Oh oh," I warned, as the front door opened, and two men stepped in from the cold. "It's Moody and Ogilvy!"

Charlie spun toward the entrance and groaned. Shelby's gaze followed him.

He spluttered. "Charlie, I can't be having this conversation with you."

"What conversation? I thought I was watching the game and you came to question me about my whereabouts at a certain time of a teenager's death. What time was that again?"

"One a.m.," Shelby whispered as the two men spotted him across the room and pushed their way forward.

"This is an interesting little gathering," the older of the men sneered, stopping in front of Shelby and looking down his nose. "You're not drinking on the job, are you?"

The tips of Shelby's ears reddened as he discreetly pushed the glass away. "I was just questioning a potential suspect on his whereabouts. Trying to stay on top of the case before the murderer gets out of town."

"Shouldn't you be doing this at the station?" Moody retorted.

"I don't see why the location matters. It's not a formal interrogation."

"So, what was the answer," Ogilvy asked, his nose wrinkled as he looked at Charlie.

"Charlie has an alibi and witnesses to prove it," Shelby informed them.

Their chests deflated as their jaws tensed.

"I suggest you check his alibi and question those witnesses, Shelby. We wouldn't want an unreliable source to allow a killer to walk free, would we?"

Shelby tensed as he pushed up to standing. "That will never happen in my town. Now, if you boys will excuse me, I'm going home. I've dealt with enough crap for one day."

"I thought you were working a double shift today?" Moody queried. "At least that's what you were moaning about this morning."

Shelby's shoulders dropped as he let out an exhausted breath. "I forgot about that," he mumbled quietly. He then lifted his face to the detectives and spoke up. "I meant I'm going home to get some lunch before I head back to work." He dropped some bills on the bar top to pay for the bottle he and Charlie had consumed and then pushed past the detectives as he made his way out the door. Ogilvy whispered a private joke to Moody, and they laughed as he slapped his colleague on the back.

Watching Shelby's stooped posture, my heart squeezed with compassion. His profession wasn't easy. He tried his best to keep Dandelion Ponds safe, which I was learning more and more each day was extremely difficult. It was a job he did with dignity, and one he didn't get enough credit for.

"What awful men," I muttered, making a mental note to ask Frank how to scare people. Only my attention was diverted as a loud pop sounded behind Charlie and Ana appeared looking flushed and happy with herself.

"Charlie, I need you back at your mom's house," she announced.

"Why?" he asked, watching the retreating backs of the two most disliked men in the room.

"I found him."

"Who?" I asked.

"Idris. The computer genius I was telling you about."

11

I gulped, snapping my lips hard together. After all, staring open mouthed at a guy wasn't a good look, right?

Idris lifted his hand in a wave, looking down at us through his dark lashes that if he was full bodied, I was sure would have left shadows on his cheeks. His dark skin glowed, his brandy-colored eyes sparkled with mischief, and his sexy stubble made my knees feel rubbery.

"Hi, everyone." His deep baritone voice brought a sigh to my lips which earned me a glare from both Charlie and Logan.

"Hi, Idris," Dorothy cooed, smoothing her woolen jacket as she smiled up at him. "It's so lovely to meet you."

"Pleased to meet you." Charlie nodded in way of a greeting.

"I've brought Idris up to date," explained Ana. "And he tells me that with the right access he can recover everything."

"Well, maybe not everything, but certainly a lot." He smiled, and I giggled. "I just need a good set of hands."

"I bet you do," cooed Dorothy, making me giggle even harder.

Charlie scoffed. "I have the hands you need."

Oh boy. Did he ever!

"Great. Now all we need is the access to the computer," Idris finished.

"What's going on?" Dorothy asked. I'd forgotten she hadn't been a part of that planning. As Charlie brought her up to date, she paled.

"You can't possibly think you're going to break into the police station?" she asked.

"Mom, don't worry. I'll be fine."

"Charlie! No. You can't."

"Only if I can't convince Shelby to help me."

"Oh my, I can't listen to this." Dorothy's hand shook as she placed it on the cushion.

"Yeah, it's probably best you don't know. That way if I get caught, you won't be an accessory."

"Just promise me you'll be careful?" she pleaded.

"Always."

"Okay then. I'm going to continue my research into how we can wake you up, Daisy. After all, the sooner that happens, the better."

Dorothy sat back heavily on the couch and picked up the book, turning the volume on the television to high. Her shoulders relaxed as the sounds of the three p.m. news bulletin broke through the awkwardness that had descended on the room.

"Tonight is a once in a century lunar eclipse," the news reader called. "So, when you're out there celebrating the beginning of a new year, make sure you look up. It's not something you want to miss." He chuckled.

"Charlie, we're running out of time," I warned, panic jumbling my thoughts. "I…I don't know that I can do this."

His gaze moved to meet mine. "I know. But you've got this, Daisy. We're going to find who killed Logan so that you can do your magic. Once we know the exact movements of Amethyst's plan we can put our heads together and figure out how to defeat her. Now, we'd better make our way back to the police station to see what we can learn." The chair scraped on the floor as he pushed it backwards and stood, determination tensing his jaw.

The Mustang's low rumble drowned the radio, as Charlie negotiated our way across town. He was deep in thought, his brow creased and his jaw flexing. I figured those thoughts weren't good ones. Not that I could blame him. My thoughts weren't much better. The weight of the new year was pressing down on me, and it felt like we were wading through mud, as the stroke of midnight zoomed closer. I chewed my thumbnail as I stared out the window, watching as Dandelion Ponds prepared itself for the festivities, unaware of Amethyst's plans.

The snow ploughs had shoveled the snow alongside the footpaths, the local park was being transformed into a firework display, and a truck driver unloaded a delivery to the bar which looked like they were stocking up on champagne. A longing filled my soul as I wished I were able to see in the new year at The Weed Killer, enjoying a drunken rendition of "Auld Lang Syne" with my friends.

Since my coma I'd learned a lot about my life. Far more than I'd known when I was conscious. I'd lost a lot of friends in the last few months, but those I'd gained had proven to me they were the best kind, and once I woke, I knew I would surround myself with them. I just hoped when I did regain consciousness, I'd remember those who were still among the living as well as still be able to see those who had passed to this in-between life and death place.

I glanced to my left, noting Charlie's ever watchful eyes, as Ana, Logan, and Idris were all in the back. More than once I'd caught her flicking her long hair over her shoulder as the toe of her Louboutin jiggled impatiently. Neither man was paying her any attention as Logan stared blankly out of the window and Idris tapped on his phone.

"Idris, what can you see on there?" I asked, nodding toward the device he held as if his life depended on it. But then maybe it had.

"Nothing," he replied, his eyes downturned. "It doesn't work in the afterlife."

"Then why do you keep checking it?"

"In the hope that may change."

"But surely you know it's not going to, so why not put it in your pocket?"

"When I was alive it was my entire life. If I wasn't connecting with those on the internet though gaming, I was hacking into systems that seemingly couldn't be hacked." He lifted the phone and shrugged. "I don't know how to put it down."

"But you're missing out on everything around you," I commented, noting little Jesse Smith in the park nearly knock out his older brother with a snowball.

"I guess so, but this is all I know."

"What about a partner? Did you have someone close?"

"Oh yeah. But I only knew her as her avatar?"

"Huh?"

"Her online alter ego," he explained.

"I know that, but what do you mean that's the only way you knew her?"

"We'd never met."

"Why not?" Ana asked, her eyebrows arched.

His cheeks hollowed as he sucked them in. "I…I was never very good at life," he admitted. "This way was so much easier."

"But you would have had women, or men for that matter, throwing themselves at you," Ana stated.

"Ummm, not really."

"But look at your eyelashes! I know people who would kill for those." She finished on a breath.

"You weren't killed for them, were you?" I asked.

"No. That was because I was hacking into a system I really shouldn't have been in, and I got caught by some not so nice characters."

"That's terrible." Ana seemed shocked. "Sure, you shouldn't have been doing what you were doing, but killing you was extreme."

"It's okay," Idris added. "I got them back for what they did to me."

"How did you do that?" I asked.

Idris beamed. "During my time in this place I've learned to move certain objects, and I may or may not have used that skill to scare the bejeezus out of the guy who killed me." He barked with laughter as Ana looked on, her eyes huge.

"Can you teach me how to do that?" she asked, her voice full of awe.

"Yeah, sure. It's not like I have a lot else to do."

The car slowed, pulling my attention toward Charlie. He turned into the parking lot of the police station.

"I visit this place far too often," he mumbled, stopping the car in a marked space.

I thought it best not to mention that was only since he'd met me. Instead, I waited for him to open the door and get out before hopping over the seats and following him. For the benefit of anyone watching, he made a show of zipping his jacket while the other three followed. Then he shut the car door and beeped it locked before leading the parade inside.

The station was a hive of activity. Officer Madison was busy shuffling through paperwork while the two plainclothes detectives stood behind her looking impatient. Shelby was tapping away at his keyboard, giving them the occasional stink eye.

"What have you done with it, Shelby?" Detective Ogilvy barked.

"I told you, I don't have it. I never did," Shelby snapped back.

Madison reached for the computer mouse and bumped a glass of water. It splashed against the detective's pants, leaving a large wet patch in its wake.

Ogilvy lurched back, cursing. "This place is a circus!"

Shelby smirked before noticing Charlie standing near the counter. Jumping into professional mode, Shelby pushed his chair backwards over the vinyl floor. He stood and approached the counter.

Ogilvy used his sleeve to wipe his wet pants, while Moody snatched a handful of files.

"Let's go back to the scene and take another look," the younger detective said, tapping the shoulder of his colleague with the paperwork.

Ogilvy sneered down at Madison. "I suggest you find a cloth and clean that mess up." They both turned before stepping past us and exiting the way we had come.

Madison's face flushed as she rushed to move vital paper from the flow of the spill. Once she was happy everything was safe, she scurried in the opposite direction to the detectives and disappeared into what I knew was the small kitchen.

I'd only once spent time in the cells, back when I was a teenager and Lilli had led me into trouble. Thankfully, an hour was all I needed to learn I never wanted to be on the wrong side of the law ever again.

"Charlie, what can I do for you?" Shelby asked, as clanging from the kitchen echoed toward us.

"Is she okay?" Charlie asked, nodding in the direction of the noise.

Shelby released a long breath and pinched the bridge of his nose. "Yeah, it's not the first time today she's done that. It was however, the first time she's wet Ogilvy's crotch." His smirk twitched at the corners of his lips.

"I'm sure he deserved it," Charlie finished.

Shelby looked like he wanted to answer but chose to move the conversation on. "What brings you here?"

Charlie shuffled one foot to the other.

"Don't be scared," I whispered in his ear. "We're all here to back you up."

His gaze flicked to me before he swallowed hard. "I was wondering if we could talk in private?"

"Does this have anything to do with the case?"

"It has everything to do with it."

"Charlie, I can't divulge any information with you. I've already said too much. My advice is that you should consult your lawyer."

"Shelby, please. I have a lot to tell you, and I know it can help solve Logan's murder."

"Will it tell me who did it?"

"Quite possibly."

"Then start talking."

Charlie looked toward the clanging still coming from the kitchen area. "I'd rather we were alone."

"What can't you say in front of another officer?"

"It's not what I can say, but what, with your help, I can show you."

Shelby's eyebrows arched as he leaned back on his heels. "With my help?"

"Ahuh. I can help you retrieve the missing CCTV footage from the hospital."

Trent Shelby's mouth dropped open as he moved his hands to the counter. "How exactly are you going to do that?"

"I need access to your computers."

Shelby shook his head. "Not possible. And since when have you become a computer expert?"

Charlie released a long breath. "I'm worried you'll never believe me."

"Try me."

Charlie looked toward the kitchen as the clanging had ceased. "I want to—but not here."

"You asked for access to our computers. This is where they are." He swept his hand through the air toward the monitors sitting on the desks behind him.

"Fair point." Charlie nodded toward the kitchen and Madison. "But we're not alone, and I'm sure you have cameras watching our every move."

"We sure do. And they aren't something I can turn off without questions coming my way."

Idris stepped forward and jumped the counter, gazing at one of the screens. "That's not a problem," he called. "Charlie you can stay on that side of the counter and shout my directions to him."

Charlie nodded and repeated the idea.

Shelby stared at Charlie as if he were looking for answers. Finally, his shoulders dropped and he exhaled. "I have no idea why I'm agreeing to talk to you about this, other than I think you have some answers to a few of my questions."

"So, you'll agree to let me look."

"No, but I'm agreeing to listen to why you think I should. Give me a minute, and I'll send Madison on a mission." Shelby pushed off the counter and shuffled toward the kitchen where we heard muffled voices. Seconds later Madison made her way to her desk, retrieved her jacket, and exited the building, her smile large and fast. Charlie nodded as she passed, and I noticed her misstep before she waved back at him.

"What did you tell her?" Charlie asked as the door swung closed.

"I gave her an early mark. The detectives have been hard on her today. She deserves the break. Speaking of which, Ogilvy and Moody will be back within the hour, so you'd better start talking."

Charlie sucked in a deep breath and launched into the events of the last few weeks. By the time he'd finished, Shelby's mouth was wide open, his eyes were huge, and he looked like he needed to sit down.

"You're trying to tell me you have a band of spirits following you around?" he asked Charlie. "One of whom is a computer genius?"

"Ahuh. It sounds crazy, I know."

"Crazy? I should be calling the hospital and having you admitted!"

"I can prove it."

"That I'd like to see."

"Daisy is here. What would you like to ask her?"

"The spirit of Daisy Montgomery is standing beside you?" Shelby's brows drew together as he shoved his hands in his pockets.

"Yep. So, feel free to ask her anything, and I'll translate."

"Okay." Shelby shook his head. "Then tell me who is in my cell out the back."

I smiled at Charlie and hurried along the hallway to the holding cells. I yelled, "Benjamin Brown!"

Charlie repeated my words, and Shelby jolted, his gaze darting around the room. "That was a good guess. Okay, how many fingers am I holding up behind my back?"

Ana made it there before I did and called out, "Two. And that's just plain rude."

Charlie grinned.

I was making my way back into the room when a personal message on Shelby's phone dinged. The screen lit up, and I read the words from his wife.

"I think he's fighting with Mrs. Shelby," I called, stepping toward them. "His wife is apologizing."

Charlie hurriedly explained the message. Shelby reddened as he snatched his phone off the desk and swiped the screen. I read over his shoulder.

"Oh dear," I said. "This looks pretty private. Ask him to open a different message."

"I'm sorry you and your wife are arguing over who was responsible for the mix-up at the bank, but Daisy has asked if you can open another message, and she'll read it back to me."

Shelby took a shuddery breath, as he spun in circles, his eyes wide.

"What the..." he mumbled before stabbing at the screen. A message from Brayden from The Weed Killer flashed before me.

"Brayden is organizing another card night and wants to know if Shelby would like to lead a team," I read.

Charlie repeated it, and Shelby paled.

"No way," he mumbled. " Can, can you see a reflection somewhere?"

"No. Daisy read it."

Shelby gulped. "Let's try another one," he pronounced, once again swiping at the screen.

"Don Walters wants to know if he can borrow Shelby's skis for a trip he's taking to Canada next month. Apparently his broke after he fell on the last trip, and he never got around to buying new ones." I shrugged. "Lucky Don Walters. I wouldn't mind a trip to Canada about now."

Once Charlie repeated the message Shelby sat heavily on the nearest chair and dropped his phone on the desk. After a beat he turned to Charlie, his mouth slack as he slowly shook his head.

"Just so I get this straight," he said quietly, "you're travelling around town with how many spirits?"

"At the moment? Four." Charlie lowered his voice as he leaned closer to the counter. "Between you and me, I can't wait to get rid of Logan. He's grating on my nerves."

Logan huffed and crossed his arms over his chest. "You think I'm enjoying this?" he spat.

Charlie rolled his eyes in Logan's direction but remained silent.

"Logan Cutter is here with you now?" Shelby asked.

"Ahuh."

"Then why not ask him who the murderer is?"

"Do you really think I haven't already done that? He didn't see who did it."

Shelby audibly exhaled. "Which is why you want the computer hacker to tell me what to do in order to find the deleted CCTV footage?"

"Yes. At least we hope he can."

"Am I dreaming?" Shelby asked, rapidly staring into every corner of the room as if looking for someone.

"No. Daisy can see your dreams, and she says they don't usually involve work," Charlie improvised.

Shelby blushed and snapped his head toward Charlie. "She cannot see my dreams."

"I could if I wanted to." I wiggled my eyebrows.

"She's intrigued now," Charlie replied.

Shelby jolted and pulled the computer keyboard toward him. He then jiggled the mouse, and the screen flashed to life. Idris grinned and started to ask a few questions, which Charlie repeated. As Shelby tapped the corresponding keys, it didn't take long for me to get bored of the process.

"Hey, Charlie," I said, remembering an earlier conversation. "When he's done, can you ask him to search the records for Amethyst's daughter? If we believe the killer is one and the same person, then this can be over before it begins."

Charlie nodded before repeating another of Idris's commands. I gave Shelby his due. Other than the pallid color of his skin, he sure was taking all this in his stride.

Ana moved in alongside Logan and dropped her lips to his ear. Moments later Logan smiled, and they both moved to the other side of the room where they sat on the plastic chairs propped against the wall, their heads close in deep conversation.

"Does Shelby know what the latest murder weapon was?" I

asked, as the computer speak sounded like a foreign language to me.

Seconds later Shelby replied, "It was a sharp object. I think it's a scalpel, but I'm still waiting on the autopsy report to verify that."

I was about to reply when Charlie's phone rang, and he pulled it from his pocket.

"Hi, Mom. No, I'm still at the station. Ahuh." I pushed my ear next to the phone wanting to hear what she had to say. Charlie narrowed his eyes. "Daisy, can I chat to my mom in private please?"

"Is Daisy there?" I heard Dorothy call.

"Yes. She's trying to eavesdrop on our conversation."

"Put me on speaker. I need to talk to her too," Dorothy commanded.

Charlie did as asked, and seconds later Dorothy's voice drowned out Idris and held everyone's attention.

"I know what we need to do to wake Daisy up," she continued. "I need you to meet me at the hospital in half an hour."

My stomach flipped, and I gasped. "Really?" I beamed.

Logan stood and walked toward me as Ana scowled.

Charlie's smile momentarily matched mine before a frown pushed it aside.

"Mom, I'm with Shelby. He's going to help us, but we have to do it now. He can't see Idris, so I need to be here."

"Then I'll collect Daisy on the way. You stay with Shelby and solve this. The sooner we get this mystery behind us, the sooner we can all get on with our lives."

"But I wanted to be there when Daisy wakes up."

"Charlie, stay and do what you need to do. You'll have plenty of time to connect with Daisy when she's back with the living."

"No, I don't like it. It's important that I'm there."

"The spell is going to take some time. It's possible you can do what you need to do and still make it to the hospital in time.

Now, Daisy, be out the front of the station in five minutes. I'm on my way."

Charlie's hand shook as he held the phone in front of him, his eyes bulging and his breath short.

I reached out to him and allowed my heat to seep into him as he ended the call.

"It's okay, Charlie. I'd like you there too, but your mom's right. We're running out of time today, but once this is all behind us, we have the rest of our lives to—"

"What if you don't remember me?" He cut in, stepping away from the others as he ran his fingers through his hair.

"How could I not?" I leaned into him, only stopping as our souls connected. My heart squeezed, and from the way his pupils dilated, I knew he felt the same. "See. There's no way I can forget that."

He nodded as emotions fought in the smoky depths of his eyes. "Daisy, I…I—"

"Charlie!" Shelby shouted across the room. "We've got it. What do I do now?"

As Logan paced the room, Idris stood impatiently behind Shelby's shoulder calling instructions he couldn't hear. The clock struck six p.m., and we all knew our time was limited. Unless we stopped her, Amethyst's plan would be in place by midnight.

"Two seconds," Charlie called to him before holding his hand out to me. "The least I'm going to do is to see you safely to Mom's car."

I accepted his gesture, my hand floating through his. "Not long until I'll be able to hold this properly," I gushed as excitement flipped in my belly. My heart rate picked up, and I wondered what the nurses at the hospital would be thinking.

We stepped out of the station together and waited for Dorothy to pull her car to a stop alongside Charlie. "I'm sending Ana with you," he said, his tone adamant. "If you need me, she can get to me quickly."

"Your mom has a phone," I teased. "She can call you just as easily." To be honest I didn't really want Ana with me. Waking up felt intimate, and her face wasn't the first I wanted to see. In fact, it wasn't even the second.

"Don't argue," he warned as he opened Dorothy's car door. "I'll give you ten minutes, and then I'll get her to meet you there."

I smiled before taking a seat alongside Dorothy as Alfie yapped from the back seat. I wanted Charlie to be with me when I woke. I wanted to hold his hand, and to feel his breath on my cheek. I knew it was going to happen and a desire to run to the hospital took control. The sooner we got this started the sooner we could be together.

Yet fear nagged at the corners of my mind. What if it didn't go to plan? As it stood, I needed to stop Amethyst tonight, but how was I going to do that? Everything suddenly felt more real than it ever had before. My life was about to change, and I hoped I was ready for it.

Charlie held the door, leaning in close as his gaze held mine, his heat burning me, an unspoken spell connecting us.

"See you on the other side, Charlie."

"I'll be looking forward to it." His grin flashed before he blew me a kiss.

12

*L*ooking down at myself I could see my color was returning. My oxygen tubes had been removed, but I still had an IV canula inserted in my arm and a catheter in a place I didn't want to think about. The sheets were pulled tight across my body, and my head was propped on a pillow. And if I wasn't mistaken a small smile played at the corners of my lips.

"So how is this going to happen?" I asked Dorothy once nurse Amanda had closed the door behind her. Ana stood near the wall, her sneer visible across the room, Logan standing alongside her, his arms folded, silently lost in his own thoughts.

Dorothy dropped her bag on the bedside table and unzipped it, both forearms momentarily disappearing within its depths as she retrieved a small mortar and pestle. A second dive brought with it a bag of vegetable greens.

"Well, first of all I'm hoping you're not allergic to basil and rosemary." She looked to me for confirmation.

"Not that I know of."

"Good. That would have put a spanner in the works, as they are the main ingredients to my spell."

"Is that what that is?" I asked as Dorothy opened the bag of greens and placed them in the mortar.

"Yes. These are from Amethyst Alexander's greenhouse, so I hope they work and aren't poisonous plants in disguise."

My mouth dropped open. "How did you get them?"

Dorothy shrugged. "I broke in and stole them. I could have purchased some from the grocery store, but I thought these would be more powerful."

"Oh my goodness! You're lucky you didn't get caught!"

"Yeah, well my cat, Percival, kept lookout for me and gave me the heads up when she was coming."

Dorothy used the pestle to pound the herbs into a paste.

"That looks disgusting." Ana wrinkled her nose as she peered at the mixture.

"Well, I'm not finished yet. I'm also adding in coco, cinnamon, ginger, and lemongrass." Dorothy stirred the mortar clockwise all while chanting under her breath. "Now Daisy, I need you to come and lie on the bed. Align yourself as best you can."

I whispered my own prayers as I wiggled into place, and the monitors relayed my excitement.

"That's a good sign." Dorothy smiled, noting the erratic tune they played. "Now I'm going to tie your hand to your spirit with this black cord." She pulled a long black leather cord from the bag and proceeded to tie it around my wrist. "Try not to move from now on. I don't want to give this any reason not to stick."

Alfie turned three concentric circles on the bed alongside me and placed his head on my chest. Ana took a large step backwards. Logan moved in beside my bed, his eyes filled with fear.

"Don't worry," I whispered to him, unable to hide my excitement. "It's all going to be okay."

He gulped as he reached for my hand. "I know. I'm happy you're going to wake. I'd just imagined this moment to be different."

"Yeah, me too. But it is what it is, and if Amethyst's dreams are going to come true then I need to wake before midnight."

"What are you going to do to stop her?"

"I honestly have no idea what's going to happen after the next minute, but whatever it is, I'm prepared to tackle it."

"Daisy, I need you to lie still," Dorothy pressed.

"Sorry." I wiggled until I was comfortable as she continued to tie my hand. "What does that do?" I asked as she tightened the cord.

"It's part of my binding spell. I want to join your spirit and your body together once again, and I want it to stay bound, which is why I need you to be still. The rosemary and basil are there to keep you awake, and the others are there to speed up the spell."

"Do you believe this will work?" I asked quietly.

"I've never performed it before so I can't make any promises. But I hope it will."

I nodded as she chanted quietly, both of her hands engulfing mine. "Universe, I'm binding Daisy's spirit and her body once again. Please help me." Squeezing me tight, her lips moved over her silent requests. Once she'd finished, she released her hold and studied my sleeping face. "Now, Daisy, I'm going to place the herbs in your mouth. This is the part where it's imperative you do not move. Everything must align perfectly. Understood?"

I nodded.

Dorothy used her fingers to scoop the mixture from the mortar as she leaned over me, her grimace firmly set.

"Dorothy, wait," I called urgently, sitting up. She halted. "I just need to say something. In case I don't remember anything when I wake up."

She relaxed back and gave me a small smile. Ana rolled her eyes; Logan tensed his jaw.

"Thank you," I started. "Thank you for everything you have done for me. I'm not close with my family, and the support and friendship you and everyone else have shown me means more to me than I can ever tell you."

"It's been my absolute pleasure, Daisy."

My gaze darted to Logan, and I lowered my voice, leaning sideways into Dorothy's personal space. "If I don't remember Charlie, can you perform a secret spell on me to help me? I don't want to lose him. Or any of you for that matter." The truth was I wouldn't miss Ana, but it felt mean to say that out loud.

"I promise you I will do everything I can help keep you two together. You're good for him," she whispered.

My heart monitor played a happy tune as I smiled.

"Now we have to hurry up," Dorothy continued. "The clock is ticking."

"I'm scared." The words rolled from my tongue before I could stop them.

"What of?"

"Everything. At the moment my body sleeps without a care in the world, but Logan's right. When I wake, I need to stop Amethyst. How am I going to do that?"

"The same way you've done everything else over the last few weeks—with us by your side."

Tears welled as I considered her words. She was right. With Charlie I could do anything.

"Okay. Let's do this." I grinned and laid back against the pillow as Dorothy parted my lips and placed the mixture from the mortar into my mouth.

The bitter taste took my breath away as she started to chant her spell.

"Daisy Montgomery, I bind thee to your spirit. May your body and soul be one again. Daisy Montgomery, I bind thee to your spirit. Your spirit and your body are to be one again." She continued to chant, her tone almost hypnotic. As I listened to her words, my breathing slowed, and I felt myself relax. It was as her voice drifted into the distance, I fell into a delicious sleep.

I'd been dreaming wild dreams filled with adventures and solving crimes alongside the most glorious man I had ever met. It was one of those dreams you wanted to sink into, to spend the day in bed and just relive it over and over again.

But a persistent nagging in the back of my head encouraged me to wake up, to face the day and whatever it brought with it. I fluttered my eyelids and waited for my little dog, Alfie, to greet me good morning.

But instead of being surrounded by my home, I was faced with a white room. The walls were bland and cold, the air smelled of disinfectant, and the sounds of monitors beeped in my peripherals.

A small yap sounded as Alfie sprang from my chest and started to lick my chin. I laughed and attempted to swat him away, but my arm was bound to the bed.

"What the...?" I cursed, as I wiggled the black cord repeatedly. My arm felt heavy, and my thoughts waded through mud.

"Hold still. I'll untie you." The woman from my dream moved forward, her smile as bright as her crocheted sweater. "Oh, Daisy, it's so good to have you here."

I frowned. "Dorothy?" I knew this woman, yet I didn't. How?

She nodded as she gently touched my arm, undoing the cord, and tears filled behind her lashes.

"The nurse is coming." The familiar tones of my fiancé, Logan, were music to my ears.

"Logan? Logan is that you?" I asked, lifting my head from the pillow for a closer look. I needed something familiar to ground me, to get my bearings, and shake off the fatigue.

He leaned close, his eyes locked onto mine, yet his presence looked dull.

"I'm here, Daisy," he said as Dorothy moved aside.

"You look...pale," I added. My weight fell against the soft pillow, my neck already tired from the exertion.

He sighed. "I have a lot to tell you, but right now the nurse is coming, so I need you to not mention Ana and I are here."

"Why?" I noticed the glamazon eyeing me suspiciously as she stood behind his shoulder.

"I'll explain later. Promise me? Please." His eyes pleaded as he looked into my soul.

I nodded, wondering if I'd actually fallen back to sleep and was dreaming once again.

Dorothy hurriedly tucked the cord in her pocket as the door swung open and the happy faces of a nurse wearing navy blue scrubs hurried toward me, her dark eyes glistening.

"Well, well, look at you." She smiled as she pressed a few buttons on the equipment alongside my bed. As she placed some equipment on my finger, I noted her name tag read Amanda. "I saw your monitor at the station and noted the changes. I was hopeful you were back with us but didn't want to get my hopes up. Doctor Ingram will be so happy."

I attempted to sit up again, but she placed a hand on my shoulder to stop me. "Don't be in a rush," she warned. "It'll take some time."

"Amanda, is she okay?" Dorothy asked.

The nurse turned to her. "She will be. When patients first wake, they are usually only with us for a short while before falling back to sleep."

"Will she slip back into the coma?"

Amanda shook her head. "It's unlikely, but I'll put a call through to the doctor and she'll follow up with an examination. Daisy has a lot of catching up to do, but we don't want to push her recovery. Small steps." Her brow lowered on the last words as her tone was filled with warning.

"Understood." Dorothy nodded.

"Charlie is going to be so happy when he gets the call with the news you're back with us," Amanda announced, tapping a few keys on a mobile workstation..

Charlie? That name stirred emotions deep within.

"I'm going to call him in a few minutes," Dorothy added, her smile large. "I'm sure he'll be here as soon as he can be."

"Sorry, Dorothy," warned Amanda. "I understand he'll want to see her, but we mustn't push Daisy too hard. She's been through a lot and has to take the time to come back to us properly."

"Of course. Well then, I'm sure he'll be here as soon as he's allowed."

Amanda smiled her agreement, finished her notes, and then strutted from the room.

Once she was gone, my attention locked onto Logan.

"Care to bring me up to date with what's been happening?" My voice was laced with weariness, but I swallowed against my dry mouth and took a deep breath.

Logan gulped, then launched into the events of the last few weeks.

"Hang on." I put my hand up as he recounted how Charlie was at the station with Idris trying to uncover who the killer was. I screwed my eyes shut, recalling a recent memory. "I remember a lot of this."

"Ahuh."

"But it was all a dream! Lilli and Lucas and Mrs. Baker. They're all okay, right?"

Dorothy and Logan both shook their heads as my heart cracked. "Please, no."

"I'm sorry, Daisy," cooed Dorothy, placing her hand over mine. "You have so much to digest."

My gaze held Logan's. "So, you're really…?" I couldn't say the word as emotion clogged my throat.

"Yeah. I'm really dead."

"That's not fair," I whispered, my heart heavy as tears stung.

"Tell me about it."

I closed my eyes and allowed my thoughts to drift over everything that I had thought was a dream. As silent tears fell for those I had loved and lost, I wanted to curl into a ball and go back to sleep. Only this time I didn't want to be roaming the Ponds as a spirit. I wanted to be in a place where no one could hurt me, and my loved ones were safe.

"We're just waiting on a call from Charlie with an update on who's behind it all," Logan added.

My heart beat faster at his name. The man from my dreams with the smoke grey eyes who had the ability to touch my soul. Losing myself in his memory, sadness was pushed away by hope as I recalled how he promised to be there beside me, for every moment, good and bad.

A thought dropped as I swiped at my tears. "Wait a minute… that means…I'm a night demon?" I asked unbelievably. "And Amethyst has a plan to take over the town. And I have to save the day?" I tried to sit up in the bed, yet my body ached and I fell back against the pillow.

Dorothy grimaced, but before she could respond a pop sounded, and Frank appeared beside me.

"Oh my goodness," he screamed, his eyelashes beating his cheeks repeatedly. "You really woke up, and I missed it! Dorothy, how could you let me miss this?" He adjusted the bodice of his red sequined gown, his glare full of accusation as a woman wearing even more crochet than Dorothy appeared beside him. She lifted her wrinkled hand and beamed.

"Elsie?" I queried.

Her smile brightened, and her teeth teetered on the brink of passing her lips.

"I'm sorry, Frank, but I had to do this alone," Dorothy replied.

"Urgh! I miss all the good stuff," he complained.

I grinned at him, grateful I could still see everyone. "Frank, you look as fabulous as ever."

His ruffled feathers settled as he basked in the compliment. "I'd like to say the same to you, but I preferred the Christmas PJs to the hospital gown, and you look a little pasty." His painted fingernail pointed in my direction as he studied my face.

"I'm sure she'll look better in the morning, after she's had a good night's sleep," Dorothy warned, flinging a glare Frank's way.

I released a long breath. "I don't think I ever want to sleep again." Even though, a quick nap sounded good. The idea of snuggling into this comfortable pillow and relaxing as I chatted to my new friends was appealing.

My eyelids fluttered as the door opened, and a doctor entered the room flanked by nurse Amanda.

My first words to her were, "Do you think I'll be fit to go home soon?"—hopeful words yet doubtful all at the same time. I liked the idea of course, but my body felt weak.

"You won't be going anywhere for a while," the doctor warned, closing the gap between us. "Your body is still recovering, and it will be some time before you're strong enough to leave."

On the one hand that was music to my ears. But on the other, Amethyst had a goal to achieve before midnight struck, and despite the fact I had no idea how, it seemed it was my job to stop her.

Dorothy and her band of spirit friends all stood back as the doctor performed a few tests on me. Only when she smiled, did a collective blissful sigh travel the room.

"You're doing well, Daisy," she said, as Amanda tapped her notes into a workstation on wheels. "I'm sure you don't want to hear this, but you need to rest. In the morning we'll have a team of doctors and physio's who will start your rehabilitation and work out a path to get you home."

I bit my lip. "Will I get back to normal?"

Doctor Ingram grinned, showing me her perfect set of teeth. "I believe so—so long as you don't rush anything and do what the specialists tell you. Now," she turned to Dorothy. "I'll leave you to say goodnight, and then I'm going to ask that you let Daisy rest. It's been a big day for her."

Dorothy nodded her agreement, as Frank pouted and Logan stood by, his brow lowered, his shoulders hunched. Ana stuck her hand on her hip and rolled her eyes.

Once the doctor had left, Dorothy moved in and took my hand in hers. She leaned close and placed a kiss on my forehead.

"What about Amethyst?" I whispered.

"Don't you worry about anything," she replied. "We'll work it all out."

"But—"

"But nothing. What's meant to be will be."

A weight lifted from my soul as her warmth travelled into my hand.

"Now, you do what the doctors tell you to, and we'll be back as soon as visiting hours allow."

I drifted in and out of sleep for what felt like eternity, but it was Amanda checking my IV lines that pulled me awake.

"What is this for?" I asked, referring to the canula still inserted in my veins.

"Mostly it's hydrating you. Now that we've removed your catheter you'll start to feel more like your old self."

"I'm not sure what my old self is anymore. So much changed while I was sleeping." I looked past her to the darkness outside the window, pushing down the fear rising in my chest.

"It's going to take some time, Daisy, so don't rush it. Do what we tell you, and everything will be okay."

I nodded and pushed down my tears. As events from the last

few weeks settled in my mind, I wanted to get up and run away from here. I'd had enough of hospitals. I wanted my own bed surrounded by my own belongings and my dream catcher. Only then did I think I would start to adjust to my new life. True, not all the changes were bad. I had my new friends by my side, and it was the start of a new year. And I couldn't forget Charlie.

"Do you think I could go to the roof to watch the New Year's fireworks?" I asked, ever hopeful.

Amanda shook her head. "Sorry, but you need to stay right here until the morning. I can't have you wandering off." She laughed. "But I'll leave your curtains open, and you'll be able to see them through the window.

"Thanks." Disappointment settled, but I quickly pushed it aside, grateful I was awake and able to see them at all.

"Do you remember anything from while you were asleep?" Amanda asked, moving to adjust my pillow.

"What do you mean?" Did she know I'd been wandering with lost souls, solving murders?

"You had a few visitors. Charlie would come here almost every day and talk to you. Do you remember any of that?"

"No, not really." At least not in the way she meant.

"I'm surprised he hasn't tried to get in yet."

I shrugged remembering her warning about me resting.

"I must say you're taking the news about Logan very well," Amanda said, straightening my sheet.

I looked past her to Logan as he leaned against the wall, his eyes hooded and sad.

"He's right here with me," I replied, tapping my chest. "He'll never leave there, no matter what."

"Good. It's always good to keep those we've lost close to our hearts." She tucked my sheet tighter to my body. "Now, no wandering, okay?"

I nodded consent as the shrill sound of a phone ringing beside my bed made me jump. Amanda handed me the receiver and said,

"I have a few things I need to take care of, so I'll leave you to take your call, but I'll be back momentarily."

"Thank you," I replied before placing the phone next to my ear. "Hello."

"Daisy? It's Dorothy."

"Oh, hi."

"You need to listen to me." Urgency rushed her words, making me catch my breath.

"What's wrong?"

"Charlie just called. He's with Officer Shelby, and they've recovered the lost CCTV footage from the hospital. They saw who murdered Logan."

My heart picked up pace as I gulped. "And?"

"It was the nurse. Amanda. And they've done some digging into her background. Daisy, she's Amethyst daughter. Charlie and Shelby are on their way, but you need to get out now!"

13

"Oh my!" I looked back at Logan as I retold what Dorothy had just said. Logan began to shake as his eyes widened and his mouth dropped open.

He paled and sat heavily on the chair alongside my bed.

"I remember now," he muttered, dropping his head into his hands. "The day I was killed. I heard the noise behind me and when I spun to see who it was, she held a scalpel in her raised hand. I didn't even have time to lift my arm to defend myself."

"I guess with her training she knew what artery to aim for."

"But why did she do it?" he asked.

"Because she's Amethyst's daughter. I'm guessing that because you didn't kill me, she was told to kill you." I prided myself on at least getting the motive correct even if I had incorrectly accused Lilli.

"What do we do now? Are you in danger?"

"Charlie and Shelby are on their way here. I don't think she can hurt me because of Dad's protection spell against the Alexanders, but I think I should lock my door anyway."

"She's only half Alexander. Does her other half make it feasible?"

I gulped. "Surely if she were able to kill me she would have done it by now, which gives me some hope at least. But either way, I'm not going to risk it."

Determination can make you do incredible things and having a possible murderer just outside your door certainly made me determined. Pushing myself up to standing, I used my IV pole for support taking a moment to get my balance. My legs were weak and my first steps shaky, my breathing was shallow, and my body ached. Even so, every slow step I took closer to the door brought with it a feeling of victory.

But before I'd made it halfway across the room the door flew open, and Amanda's smile grew as she pushed a wheelchair toward me.

"Oh, look at you. Now, where do you think you're going without me?" she asked, her steps filled with determination.

"Ummm…" Think Daisy, think. "I was…ummm…I was going to the toilet," I lied, hoping I wouldn't give away the fact I knew who she was. My gaze flipped to Logan.

"Just play along with it for now," he warned, running his hands through his hair. "Once you're in the bathroom, lock the door, and wait for Shelby."

I nodded. "What's the chair for?" I asked Amanda.

Holding my arm, she helped me lower myself into it. "You really mustn't push yourself," she warned. "It takes time for you to fully recover from what you've been through. I knew you wouldn't be able to walk, so I got organized."

"I'm so sorry. I wasn't thinking…ummm, where are we going?"

Amanda stopped short of my room door, pulled the handle, and held it open with her hip.

"Isn't the bathroom that way?" I pointed toward the attached ensuite.

I twisted to face her and saw she'd retrieved a syringe from the pocket of her scrubs. Removing the cap, she grabbed for my IV tube.

Panic ripped through me, causing my throat to close and my breathing to quicken. Pushing myself up out of the chair, I yanked my arm away and attempted to distance myself from her as Logan screamed in my ear.

"What…what are you doing?" I wheezed as my legs buckled and I stumbled to the floor.

"Oh, I need to make you sleepy."

"Why?"

"Because I need to get you someplace else, and I took a wild guess and figured you wouldn't come willingly. Plans have changed, and we're now using you in tonight's ritual."

"But…but I don't understand."

She huffed. "Which bit?"

"You had no idea I was going to wake today. If I'm important then how did you know?"

"Oh, you were going anyway. Awake or asleep. You see, Mom decided that as no one had managed to eliminate you, then using your blood may just be the secret weapon she needs. It would have been so much easier if it needn't have been fresh. I could have taken some while you laid here completely unaware of what we were doing."

"What *are* you doing?" I stalled, hoping Charlie and Shelby would get here in time.

Dizziness swirled as Amanda stood over me.

"Well, if you cooperate I promise you'll get a front row seat to a once in a lifetime event. Now make my life easy and get back into the chair so I can give you this drug."

"Wh…what is it?" I looked to Logan, wishing he'd learned how to do the whole spirit jumping through space thing. But as his eyes widened and his lips trembled, I knew he felt as helpless as I did.

"Just a little concoction I stole from the operating theater.

Don't worry, I have the antidote, so you'll wake up when I'm ready."

Pulling my legs under me, I attempted to get up—not to help Amanda, but to try to get away from her.

"If I cooperate you won't need to give me the drug." And being conscious would give me the chance to find a way out.

Amanda cocked her eyebrow as she considered me. "Sorry, but I don't trust you."

She had good instincts.

"The other staff members will see you take me." My socked feet slipped on the vinyl, and I fell backward, holding the wall for support.

Amanda laughed and grabbed for my IV pole. "No, they won't. I've flooded the ward with valerian. And we both know that'll knock everyone out for hours. Now sit!" Inserting the needle into the tube, she snickered.

My world rapidly shrank, and as the lights dimmed, I gave in to the darkness, falling back to sleep.

The hard floor was cold against my back. My head pounded, and nausea swirled. My leg cramped, and I cried as I tried to stretch it, while the smell of damp concrete filled my sinuses. I blinked, trying to get my bearings, to learn where I was as memories mixed together in a vortex of color in my mind. I groaned and rolled onto my side. Freezing air hit my throat, causing me to cough.

"Daisy! Thank goodness you're waking up." Logan's voice was strong in my ear, pulling me forward. I blinked harder, wanting my eyes to adjust to the dim room.

Candlelight eerily illuminated Amanda as she knelt in front of me.

"Oh, look who's joining us," she sang. "For a minute there I was worried I may have put too many drugs in your little cocktail. Thank goodness for antidotes, right?" She giggled, clicking the cap on a syringe, and dropping it in her pocket. "What am I saying? I couldn't kill you if I tried. And believe me, I tried."

"Where am I?" I asked, ignoring her and pushing myself to sitting, noting the IV tube was gone, only the canula was left in my arm.

"We're at Logan's office building," she explained. "Getting you here was slightly more difficult than I anticipated. They must have been feeding you well while you were in a coma. You're bloody heavy."

"What are we doing here?" I ignored her comments and forced myself onto my knees and off the cold concrete. My body was weak and sore, and my mind was groggy, making every movement difficult. But Logan's voice was strong beside me, encouraging my every move.

"That's it, Daisy. You can do it. Just get up, and when she's not looking, run for the door."

I liked his theory, but the brain fog was making it difficult to come up with a plan, and my shaking legs weren't supporting the idea of running.

Amanda tutted. "Oh, come on. Surely you know why we're here. You're not stupid."

"I'm guessing Amethyst will be along shortly."

Amanda beamed. "Well done!"

"But why here exactly?" I pushed myself to standing, my knees rubbery as I took in my surroundings.

The lunar eclipse had started long ago. Partial moonlight poured in through the large windows, casting shadows as flickering light from large wicker candles danced against the walls. Amanda's breath hung in the air like tendrils of fog. She released a long sigh as if my ignorance annoyed her.

I was freezing, my hospital gown and bare feet provided no

warmth against the winter air. But I had to ignore that and focus on a way out of here.

Shivering, I slowly moved, willing my eyes to adjust to the fading light. I didn't have a lot of time before the moon was at full eclipse and we would be in total darkness right before the new year struck. My hands reached out to the concrete walls, feeling my way around the edges of the room.

Only with every step I took, the walls were pushed aside by visions of a garden filled with deadly nightshade, angel's trumpet, and English ivy. Laburnum hung over the castor oil plant which competed for space with the snake plant, and the midnight blue buds on the monkshood waited to kill. Memories of a dream burned bright, and voices long forgotten were loud in my ear.

"The Lethal Garden," I whispered, reaching for a tiny stem growing from a crack in the cement. "That's why this place is so important. It's where the night demons began."

Amanda clapped, excitedly.

"You're so good at this," she cried, her tone patronizing.

I closed my eyes. Visions of women dressed from a long-gone era surrounded by poisonous plants filtered through the fog. Conversations between them competed with each other as my attention focused on the plant one of them held tight against her chest. The petal-less stalk dotted with reddish brown flowers looked familiar, yet I had no idea what it was. Only I knew it was powerful.

Snapping my eyes open I looked down at my fingers noting the stem I'd pulled from the crack, the tiny flowers glistening under the moonlight.

Could it be?

I gasped and discreetly pushed the stem into the waistline of my panties.

Movement behind me startled me from the dream, and I spun to see Amethyst strut into the room, Lilli flanking her.

"You've done well, my child," Amethyst cooed, stopping

alongside Amanda, and pulling her close in a hug. Amethyst's long black cloak wrapped around her shoulders, and a thick silver chain holding an amulet clinked as she moved.

"Thanks, Mom," Amanda replied, her smile smug as she looked at Lilli.

"At least one of my children hasn't failed and let me down." Amethyst's dramatic makeup was striking, her skin luminescent in the moonlight. A dark high-necked shirt clung to her svelte frame, tucked into slim fitting jeans, her knee-high boots completing the look. She portrayed a woman of power, and she pulled it off.

I shrank back toward the shadows, my muscles taught and ready to run.

Lilli stood stock still, barely breathing. Our eyes connected, and for a moment I saw my best friend, the woman whom I'd grown with and shared my secrets with. But then as she blinked, the woman I'd learned she really was glared back at me.

Emotions boiled inside. Love for our friendship was pushed aside by hurt for what she had done. Sadness for what she had become gave way to anger as Logan moved behind me.

"Why didn't you stop her killing Logan?" I asked Lilli. My hand shook as I pointed at Amanda.

"Stop who?" Lilli demanded, shoving her hands into the pockets of her dark trench coat.

"Amanda. She killed Logan. Why? Why was that necessary, and why didn't you stop her? You claim you loved him, yet you did nothing to prevent his death!"

I rolled my shoulders as my muscles quivered and I fought back the urge to run and hit her. I needed to stay in control if I was to get out of this alive.

Lilli's head snapped toward Amanda, and I saw her gulp.

"Children, no fighting." Amethyst pulled herself up to her full height as she adjusted her cloak, swiping some dust from its lapel. "Lilli, once I learned how Logan was going to help Daisy escape, Amanda did what needed to be done."

"Wait a minute!" shouted Lilli. "Are you telling me she killed him?" Her shoulders tensed, her eyes wide as anger spat from their depths.

"If he'd done as asked it wouldn't have been necessary," Amanda returned, taking a small step behind Amethyst. "Honestly, I have no idea why everyone has found it so hard to kill Daisy. If I could have done it, she'd have been dead months ago. You have no idea how many doctors I've tried to influence to do it."

"It's because you're only half night demon," Lilli snarled.

"It's okay, sweetheart," Amethyst cooed, grooming Amanda by tucking her hair behind her ears. "Daisy's father's protection spell was too powerful. Once I realized that I decided instead of killing her I'm going to use her to our advantage."

"I hate you!" Lilli pushed off the balls of her feet and ran across the space, pushing past Amethyst and pummeling into Amanda. They fell with a thump in a heap of cursing and fists.

Amethyst smiled adoringly, her tinkling laughter grating on my nerves as she looked on to the consequences of her actions. But as she was preoccupied, I took the chance to step toward the door, hoping if she was distracted enough, I could put Logan's plan into place and run outside and hide.

Only Amethyst was quicker than I gave her credit for, as she glided across the floor stopping only inches from my face.

"Don't even think about it," she snarled down at me, slapping me hard across the cheek.

I stumbled, my legs weak and jelly-like.

"Leave her alone!" Logan shouted. Only it was to no avail. No one could hear him. "Daisy, look out!"

I looked up in time to see Amethyst raise her hand again, her fingers twitching as a spell whispered on her lips. She slammed her fist toward me. I ducked, her spell hitting the wall. The concrete shattered under its force.

"Ana!" Logan screamed. "Ana, can you hear me? I need you to get Charlie!"

"He's already on his way." Ana entered with a pop. "I had them divert from the hospital to here. Daisy just needs to hold Amethyst off until they arrive."

That was going to be easier said than done.

I strangled the cry in my throat as I searched the building for a weapon. Amethyst stood back, her arms wide, eyes rolled backwards as she conjured another spell. Seconds later vines sprouted from the walls, entangling my arms and legs, and pulling me tight against it. I gasped as I fought them, unsure what to do. I was out of my depth, my power no match to Amethyst's.

"Help!" I blinked rapidly, desperately trying to control my breathing while adrenalin pushed my mind to work at warp speed.

Lilli looked my way just as Amanda hit her square on the jaw, knocking her into me. Her flailing hands grasped at the vines as she fell, breaking one and freeing me from my binds. Before it could regrow, I tugged it from the wall. Desperately clawing at leaves, I continued to escape. Amethyst's mood darkened, and she screamed another curse. I ducked and it hit the foliage, poisonous oil oozing from its leaves.

Adrenaline pumped. My mind kicked into gear, and I seized the opportunity, throwing a handful of the toxic leaves at Amethyst. My aim was spot on, the oil spattering over her face, burning where it touched.

"Argh!" She launched herself toward me, the cloak giving her the appearance of flying. "You'll pay for that!"

She stopped short, her hand raised, fingers splayed just inches from my face. Her own face was contorted with rage. I took a frenzied breath as her head rolled back, and she started to chant.

Cracking concrete thundered behind me as the walls started

to crumble, and the vines advanced from within at an alarming rate. Once again it took hold of me, wrapping its tentacles around my neck and compressing my airway.

"Wait!" I wheezed, my hands scrambling to tear the vines from my throat. "The lunar eclipse! It's nearly full."

Amethyst stopped chanting, halting the vines. Her head rotated toward the window, and her smile grew as if she were enchanted by the darkness descending upon us.

I fought against the force pulling life from me, but it felt like I was drowning in quicksand. My throat constricted, my lungs burned, and fear shot through my heart. As the moonlight waned, the world turned black, and I gave in to the darkness as it consumed me.

14

$\mathcal{I}$ sat up, gasping for air. "Argh!"

"Oh, Daisy, thank goodness."

"Logan?" I blinked against the bright light stinging my retinas. "What's going on? Where am I?"

As I glanced around the room, Logan took my hand and helped me sit up.

"Am I in my bedroom?" I asked, confused as to how I got there.

"It seems that way," he replied, following my gaze.

"But what am I doing here? Last I remembered I was in the office building, and a darkness pulled me toward it. I didn't want to give in, but it was too strong for me." My lip trembled as I touched my throat.

"Daisy, can you feel me?" Logan gently took my hand and placed it in his. His palm was cold as it slid against mine, his emerald-green eyes sad as they searched my soul.

"Why can I feel you now?" I asked, my breath quickening.

"I don't really understand any of it." His head hung low as his thumb traced circles on my wrist.

"Am I dead?" I whispered, my breath stolen as tears brimmed

160

behind his lashes.

He repeatedly squeezed my hand as he stumbled to answer.

Gulping, he took three slow breaths. "You're on the path, but there's still time to change that. Only it's up to you."

"What do you mean?"

"When we pass there's a small window of time where we can go back and continue to live. You just have to choose it."

Recent memories of Amethyst Alexander pounded in my skull and caused my legs to shake and my heart to race. I'd felt weak as I faced her, despite the desire to run and hide making my body move. If I went back, I would have to confront her again, and I didn't think I was brave enough for that.

"But what if I don't want to?" I asked, enjoying the calm instilled by being here.

"Listen to me." His voice was filled with an urgency that made me stop. "When I was at this stage, I didn't know what to do, and I ran away from the light, scared. But I'm not letting that happen to you. You need to go back, Daisy."

My head spun, images swirling before my eyes. "What do you mean? There is no light."

"Concentrate. You'll see it. It'll take you home."

I glanced around my room, a feeling of peace filling my soul. I loved it here. It was where I felt calm and relaxed. My gaze stopped on the dream catcher above my bed, and memories of my dad rushed forward.

"I am home," I whispered.

A cry strangled in Logan's throat. "Please, Daisy. You have to go back. You have to stop Amethyst."

"Stop her from what? I don't even know what she's doing!"

"She's gaining power. Strength. And that is never a good thing for her to have."

Staring at the hand-painted daisies on my dream catcher I took a moment to settle my thoughts. I knew what Logan said was correct. Despite not knowing what Amethyst wanted once she'd increased her power, I innately knew it wasn't going to be used for good.

My dad had warned me about that family, yet why had I not listened to him? Why had I allowed Lilli to become close? I'd let him down, and the only way to make that right was to go back and stand strong against her.

But it was safe here. I felt cocooned in warmth in a place where no one could hurt me. Peace settled into my heart, and contentment sounded on my lips.

"When you passed, did you see your family?" I asked, as a lightness filled my chest at the thought I may see my dad soon.

Logan swallowed hard. "Yes. My grandad was waiting for me."

I nodded as my smile spread. "That's good. Your grandad was a wonderful man. Maybe I can see him now too."

"No, Daisy. Please, you need to go back. It's not time for you to be here yet."

"I have nothing to go back for Logan. Everything I want is here."

"You're wrong. You have Charlie." A single tear spilled over Logan's lashes, leaving a damp trail in its path.

Visions of Charlie's smoke grey eyes made me gasp. "He doesn't want me. I only make his life difficult. If I stay here, will you want me?"

"I will never stop wanting you," he whispered.

I smiled and leaned my head against his. "Despite your affection for Ana?"

Logan swiped at his tears and laughed. "She's adorable, but she's not you."

"Then let me stay. I like it here already."

Logan rubbed his thumb over my cheek, his eyes boring into mine. "Daisy, as much as I want that, you're not mine. You never were. You were always destined to be with Charlie."

"But if I go back, I have to fight Amethyst, and I'm not strong enough." My own tears spilled, and a tightness squeezed my chest.

"You are. You have more courage and strength than anyone I know. And we'll all be there with you, helping in any way we can."

Movement stirred behind him, and Elsie, Frank, and Ana stepped into view. As they moved aside, they left a man smiling at me.

I gasped.

"Dad?"

He beamed, crossing the floor toward me. "We'll never leave you, Daisy," he reassured. "We'll be right by your side the whole time."

"Oh, Dad!" I jumped up and threw myself into his arms, enjoying the feeling of safety that engulfed me. "I've missed you."

"I've missed you, too." He laughed.

I squeezed him tight as I buried my face into his chest, his familiar scent filling me with contentment. The day I said goodbye to my father had been the hardest day of my life. To have the chance to hold him one more time was something that only happened in my dreams, and I wasn't prepared to walk away from it.

"I'm never letting you go again," I cried, giving into the sobs that wracked my body.

Dad rubbed my back, reminding me of a time long ago. "Daisy, I wish it could be that way. I really do. And one day it will, I promise. But that day is not today."

"You don't understand." I sniffed, pulling back to look him in the eye. "I like it here. It's peaceful. I don't have any fear, and Amethyst can no longer hurt me. Don't you see why I need to stay?"

"I do see, but it's not your time." He wiped my tears with his thumbs and smiled gently.

"I have nothing to go back to," I argued.

"You have those who love you," Elsie encouraged.

"You're wrong. You're all wrong!" I declared. "No one has missed me since I've been in a coma. Mum barely comes to see me, and don't even get me started on Stacey! Plus, Alfie is happy with Charlie. It's like they're soul mates."

"PFMT." Ana exhaled so hard it ruffled her hair. "As much as I hate to admit it, Charlie needs you. It appears you are his soul mate after all. Not the dog!"

"Daisy, you're running out of time," Logan prodded, taking my elbow in his hand. "You need to go back now before it's too late."

"But, but—"

"I love you," he whispered, placing a delicate kiss on my cheek. "That'll never change. But you need to go."

Dad took my hands in his. Tears filled behind his lashes, and he swallowed hard, his words lost to his emotions. It was okay. We didn't need words.

I enjoyed his strength and leaned into him as he pulled me close, the rhythm of his heartbeat soothing and calm to my soul. I never wanted to move. I was a daddy's girl through and through, and I'd missed him more than I could ever admit even to myself.

"Daisy, listen to me." He pulled my shoulders back, breaking the warmth that had hugged me. "I should have told you all of this when I was alive, but I thought by not knowing you would be safe. Only I was wrong."

"It's okay. I know." I smiled. "I know we're descendants of Valeria, the first night demon."

"Yes, but what you don't know is you hold the power to defeat Amethyst. She thinks your blood will intensify the spell. Only, Daisy, your blood is the exact weapon that can destroy them. If you crush the artemisia plant and mix it with your blood, it will make you the most powerful night demon of all time. Only then can you stop her. But you need to wake up, or you won't be strong enough. I can't protect you now."

"Artemisia?" I asked.

"It's the Latin name for wormwood or mugwort. It's the plant associated with powerful women."

I nodded and removed the small stem from the waistband of my underwear. "It's a hallucinogenic compound that brings on visions and dreams." I held the small plant up for him to see. "The original garden is coming back to life. But Dad, if I go back, what do I do with it?"

"Allow the first moonlight after the lunar eclipse to fall on the leaves, then eat it."

I gulped. "But…won't that kill me?"

"No. My protection spell is still doing its job. Once the eclipse has passed though, it will wear off."

I shivered but nodded my understanding. My shoulders relaxed, and my breath evened out. I didn't want to leave, but deep down I knew I had to. With that kind of strength Amethyst would destroy Dandelion Ponds and everyone in it. I couldn't let that happen to my friends and loved ones. As much as I didn't want it to be this way, I resigned myself to the knowledge settling in my belly and took from it the courage I needed.

Holding Dad's gaze, I smiled.

"Good girl. Now go get 'em."

"Dad? Will I see you once I wake up?" Tears prickled as need bubbled up inside me.

"No. I've moved on, Daisy. You have no idea what it took to get here now." He grinned. "But when your time comes, I'll be right here waiting for you. Only that is a long, long time away. You have a lot of living to do first."

I bit back my cry as the moisture fell over my lashes, and a pain started around my heart.

"What about you, Logan? Will I still see you?"

He looked toward Ana before nodding. "Yeah, I'm not ready to move on just yet. But it's time you tell the world who really killed me and why. I'm sorry, Daisy, but it has to be you. You're the only one who can defeat Amethyst and make Amanda pay for what she did."

"You have everything you need, Daisy," Dad encouraged.

"I don't have you," I whispered.

"I gave you everything I had, and besides with Frank, Elsie, Logan, and Ana there to back you up, what more do you need?" He winked as his mischievous grin exploded.

"You make it sound so easy." I laughed despite the dread that sat heavy on my shoulders.

All humor left the room as we considered what would happen next, and I took a moment to enjoy my loved ones.

Logan was right—the world needed to know who killed him. And Amethyst needed to pay for what she had done. And I was pretty sure Charlie was on his way, and he didn't have the knowledge of how to defeat her. Whether he wanted me in his life or not, I needed him.

I released a ragged breath. "Well, I guess if I fail, I'll end up back here anyway."

Only I didn't want to fail. I wanted her to leave us alone, and if it had to be me who stopped her, then I knew exactly what I had to do.

I blinked in the darkness. A cold breeze whipped my hair into my eyes as a rat scratched its way across the cement floor. The invisible scent of recently extinguished candlewax hung in the air as an eerie silence echoed loudly.

My gaze darted to the window, and the three women staring at the eclipse were silhouetted against the blood red occlusion of the moon.

Snatching the opportunity before Amethyst once again started to chant, I freed myself from the vines still binding me. My heartbeat was erratic, my breath coming in short, sharp bursts as I silently scurried to the opposite side of the room. Only when I was out of their grasp did I take a second to admire the night sky, feeling power fill me with hope.

I had a small window of opportunity to get my thoughts together, to find a way to end this now. Pushing my back against the wall, I slowed my breathing, controlled my fear, and came up with a plan.

Amethyst tore her attention from the moon and started to bark her orders.

"Amanda, hurry and get the altar ready. We don't have a lot of time. Now where did Daisy go? I thought she was unconscious. This would have been so much easier if she was." Her neck twisted as she searched for me. "Oh! Thought you could escape, did you? Lilli, tie her up again and relight the candles. I can barely see a thing in here."

"I thought the candles needed to be extinguished," Lilli complained. "The moon was supposed to light our path."

"Yes, well, that all sounds good in theory, but right now, I'm falling over my own feet. Now hurry up for goodness' sake."

The pungent aroma of sulfur dioxide burst as Lilli struck a match, relighting the nearest candle. Her eyes were downturned, her lips in a scowl as she closed the gap between us, retrieving a black cord from her mother's bag as she moved.

Amanda lit a Wicca candle then used the tip of a black-handled blade to scratch a circle on the concrete floor.

I felt for the mugwort in my palm, replaying my plan in my mind, and willing everything to go just the way I needed it to. It was essential I pummel it into a paste all while Amethyst and her daughters were trying to destroy me.

Could I do it? As Logan, Elsie, Ana, and Frank appeared and corralled around Amethyst, a fire lit inside me, and determination flourished.

"Why are you doing this?" I asked Amethyst, as Lilli yanked

my hands behind my back. I tightened my fist and protected the mugwort, this not part of my plan.

"Because I want to rule the world, and this town is where I begin. I want it under my spell, the residents trapped to do my bidding. It will make me the greatest night demon of our era." She smiled lightly, knelt on the floor in front of the Wicca candle, and opened her grimoire. She flipped through the pages until she found what she wanted, then stopped, and inhaled deeply. "The lunar eclipse is nearly over, and I need to be ready."

Retrieving a pestle and mortar from her bag, she ceremoniously dropped herbs and oils into it, while chanting quietly under her breath.

Lilli gripped my wrists and leaned in close to my ear. "Make them pay for Logan," she whispered, dropping the cord to the floor.

My skin tingled as I twisted to face her. Our eyes met briefly, and even in the dim light I could see the hatred she had boiling inside. In that moment I knew she really had loved Logan.

I gave a small nod before she moved closer to her mother.

Amanda finished setting the stage as I clutched the mugwort tightly.

"Get Daisy in the circle," Amethyst screamed.

Amanda rushed at me, grabbing my arm and half dragging me across the floor as I fought to get my feet under me in time. The mugwort slipped from my fingers, and I cried out against the pain.

Outside, the moon continued to glow red as the Earth blocked the moon beams from its path, but the Earth moved at a thousand miles per hour, and it wasn't going to be long before the first sliver of new light shone bright.

Amanda dumped me in front of the makeshift altar as Amethyst stood tall, raising her arms to the heavens, her spell lingering on her lips—except her words were lost as the yap of a small dog broke through the tense atmosphere, and Alfie bounded toward me, Dorothy's cat, Percival, hot on his heels.

"Guys! What are you doing here?" I cried, sitting back on my heels. "As happy as I am to see you, you need to go before you get hurt." I had enough on my plate without worrying about them. I needed them home where they were safe.

It appeared they had other ideas as instead of running toward my outstretched arms, Percival hissed and ran at Amethyst giving Alfie the distraction he needed to snatch the mugwort between his teeth and bring it to me.

"Get away, you stupid cat," Amethyst snarled, side-stepping Percival.

"Good boy," I cooed, taking the mugwort from Alfie and hoping he hadn't consumed any of it. "How did you know that's what I needed?" I gave his ears a gentle rub, taking a moment for their softness to settle my nerves and calm me, allowing me to see clearly.

Amethyst scoffed and brushed herself down before straightening her back. She reopened her arms as she started to chant. Lilli slunk back toward the exit.

Remembering Dad's words, I summoned my strength and shoved the plant between my lips, using my teeth as a mortar and pestle to grind it to a paste.

Logan, Elsie, Frank, and Ana rallied around, calling instructions to the animals.

"Percival, get her!" Frank yelled pointing at Amethyst. Percival didn't hesitate, he hunched low before pushing off his back legs and launching himself into the air. Amethyst screamed as his claws dug into her flesh, sliding down her face before he landed with a satisfied thump on the floor.

Amanda squealed as she jumped at Alfie. "Get out of here, you mangy mutt! You can't mess this up!" Only he ran between her legs, and she tripped as she rushed after him.

The light changed as the red moon faded and the black-handled blade glistened under the first rays from the light of the new moon. As Percival howled and once again attacked Amethyst's face, I seized the opportunity to grab the knife.

In one fast slice, I cut my hand and winced as fresh blood oozed from the wound. I ran to the window, holding my hand to my lips, allowing the sweetness of my blood to mix with the bitterness of the mugwort. I closed my eyes to the chaos in the room and concentrated my thoughts on the dream catcher on my bedroom wall and the tiny daisies my father had painted on it.

Ignoring the urge to gag, I held my tongue to the moonlight before swallowing the mixture. As fireworks exploded in the distance, the new year struck, and Amethyst stood still, her lips frozen in a sneer.

I smiled and opened my arms, allowing the moonlight to bathe me, as I started to chant a song my father sang to me as a child.

Deep within the night
   Find the dreams and make them right.
   May we all forget their force
   'Til the moonlight fades and night runs its course.
   With water, earth, wind, and fire
   Wipe their hearts of all desire.
   Stop all powers in the future, present and past.
   Only then the spell will be uncast

"Stop!" Amethyst screamed. "You'll take all of our power!"

"I think that's the point," Logan acknowledged.

"But it will take hers too," Elsie said.

"Good. It should remove the power of every night demon who walks the Earth. Every good, kind soul deserves to sleep peacefully without any nightmares," Frank finished.

I continued to chant, not even stopping for a breath as Amethyst rushed toward me, her movements appearing slower from the adrenalin flooding my body.

Blood pounded in my ears, my heart raced, and my vision clouded as every muscle quivered. The hair on my arms rose as a vortex of wind swirled around me, lifting me off my feet and pushing Amethyst backwards.

I stumbled on my words, and momentarily I fell until I once again concentrated on what I needed—on what I desired. Dreams flashed through my mind—those of people I never met, facing nightmares that changed their lives. My own dreams mixed with theirs until everything was a kaleidoscope of color. Fatigue and sadness weighed me down, but I could see Logan, Elsie, Frank, and even Ana standing guard, encouraging me to keep going. To put a stop to it all.

"Deep within the night
Find the dreams and make them right.
May we all forget their force
'Til the moonlight fades and night runs its course.
With water, earth, wind, and fire
Wipe their hearts of all desire.
Stop all powers in the future, present, and past.
Only then the curse will be uncast."

The moonlight continued to grow, and as the last word left my lips, I fell to the floor in a pool of perspiration, my breathing labored.

A man ran toward me, lifting my head into his lap. As he gazed down at me, the smoke grey depths of his eyes were the last thing I saw before I succumbed to the darkness. My heart filled with peace from the knowledge it was over.

15

I'd had enough of hospitals to last a lifetime, and Ward Four-B was definitely getting old. I was, however, grateful I was awake and no longer had to wear either a hospital gown or my red flannel Christmas-print pajamas. Nope, Dorothy had contacted the owners of Bloomfields department store and had somehow managed to convince them to open on New Year's Day and sell her a pair of blush-pink silk pajamas for me. I chose not to ask exactly how she had managed that, instead choosing to believe they gave up their holiday out of the goodness of their hearts.

In my head I justified it with the fact that now that night demons no longer held any power, the Bloomfields would sleep with blissful dreams minus the threat of Amethyst ruling over them. That alleviated all my guilt.

"Are you going to drink that hot chocolate or just look at it?" Frank asked, eyeing the takeaway cup Dorothy had also brought for me.

Dorothy was presently sitting in the chair alongside my bed, purple wool twisted around her crochet needle in a very complicated way.

"I'm savoring it." I smiled and lifted the cup to my lips, enjoying the sweet aroma before I took a sip. Frank scooted along the mattress until he was almost on top of Alfie, who was presently enjoying a snuggle on my legs.

"Does it taste as good as I remember?" he asked, licking his lips.

I laughed. "I'm not sure what you remember, but it's a thousand times better than I remember."

Frank sighed wistfully before the door opened and a bouquet of chrysanthemums entered room. As the door swung closed, Officer Trent Shelby appeared from behind the bouquet, his smile large.

"Good morning, Daisy. Dorothy." He nodded as he made his way toward me. He gave me a wry grin. "I hope these are okay. They're all I could get." Placing the bouquet on the overbed table, he leaned back on his heels and fiddled with the brim of his police-issue cap.

"They're lovely," I replied. "But where did you get them?" I knew my store Crazy Daisy's wasn't open for business, and I bit my lip hoping some competition hadn't opened in my absence.

"The gas station had a couple of bunches near the door. Not as good as anything you sold, but...anyway, I hope they're okay."

I slouched back against my pillow, relieved at the news.

"How are you feeling?" he asked, his eyes soft as he bounced on the balls of his feet.

"Sore. There's not a part of me that doesn't hurt, and I'm tired." It seemed defeating Amethyst and nearly dying in the process had left me exhausted. "But I'm grateful to be alive and to be able to tell the tale. Plus, they've removed all needles from my body which leaves me one happy lady."

"Good to hear."

"What brings you here, Shelby?" Dorothy asked, placing her crochet on her lap.

"Thought I'd stop by and personally give you the update on the case."

"Is Amethyst behind bars?" I asked.

Shelby shook his head and shuffled from one foot to the other "Ummm…it seems that she's disappeared."

"What?!" My body tensed, and stars danced in my vision.

"We had her in our cells but sometime this morning she… well, she vanished."

"But, but how?" I stammered. "Her powers were gone. I stripped her of them."

Shelby lifted one shoulder; his head held low. "I can only think she had some help."

"Hmmm, I wonder who that could have been?" Frank asked, checking his nail polish. Of course, Shelby couldn't hear him as it appeared despite the fact he now knew ghosts were real, it hadn't given him the powers to see any.

I spun my gaze to Frank. "What do you mean?"

"I was wondering if a particular new officer in town may have left a cell door open."

"Keating?"

"What about her?" Shelby asked me.

"Did she have anything to do with Amethyst disappearing?" I probed, picking up on Frank's accusation.

"No! No. She was with me the entire time. But…no. I shouldn't say."

"Shelby?"

"While there's an investigation into the behavior of two detectives, I'm not at liberty to divulge any information."

I gasped. "You think they did it?"

"I don't know for sure," Shelby replied. "Either way, they needed reporting for the way they treated Officer Keating." His brows knitted together as he stared at his cap.

"What about Amanda?" Dorothy asked, expertly moving the conversation in a safer direction.

"She's a whole different story." Shelby's eyes sparkled as he moved to look at Dorothy. "Thanks to Charlie...and Idris," he hurriedly added, looking around the room. "We have the CCTV footage of her caught in the act of killing Logan. Add in that she kidnapped Daisy, and she's facing some hefty time in prison."

Shelby shifted uncomfortably, and his grin faded. "I'm really sorry about Logan." His eyes glistened as he looked at me, and he swallowed hard.

"It's okay," I replied. "He's right here with me."

Shelby hurriedly looked over his shoulder as his gaze shot around the room. "Is he really?"

I laughed. "Not at this present moment in time. Actually, Dorothy, where is he? I haven't seen him since last night."

"Who knows?" she said, lifting her shoulders in a shrug. "Last I saw him, he and Ana had their heads together, and she was muttering something about showing him the sights."

"Oh. Well, I hope he's having a good time. He deserves it." I meant what I said, so why was a lump forming in my throat?

A lot had changed in the last few hours and it made me look at life in a completely new light. Sure, Logan hadn't always been honest with me, and at times he was almost deceitful, but if I looked at the situation through his eyes then I saw things differently. And I truly believed that he was going to help me. His help just came too late.

"They will come back, right?" I asked, not quite ready to let him go completely.

"I think that's a safe bet," Dorothy replied, winking at me.

"So, is, ummm, anyone else here?" Shelby asked, his gaze searching the room.

"Ahuh. Frank's right here." I jabbed my thumb at the man sitting alongside me on the bed.

"Frank?"

"Yeah. Frankincense. The drag queen of Dandelion Ponds," I explained.

"Oooh, I like that title," Frank cooed adjusting his wig, as Shelby shifted from one foot to the other, looking like he was unsure how to process that information.

Dorothy and I both laughed.

"Hey, Shelby, whatever happened with Logan's boss, Mike?" I asked, remembering our suspect list.

"What do you mean?"

"I heard there was some kind of loan shark chasing him. At the time we wondered if it was connected to Logan's murder."

Shelby nodded knowledgeably. "I looked into that. Mike told me he'd been having some weird dreams about Logan. He knew about the office building and how Logan was having financial trouble and was trying to get the funds to help him. Some brothers from a neighboring town were willing to do the loan, but Logan was killed before the deal went through. Luckily for Mike. The Marks brothers may be good for a quick loan, but fail to repay it and you'll lose a loved one. We're looking to do some undercover work to bring them to justice. It may be a job for a few of your spirit friends." Shelby beamed. "I could do with some inside knowledge."

"Pick me! Pick me!" Frank bounced on his toes.

"Looks like you have a volunteer." I grinned. "Let me know when you're ready, and I'll interpret for you."

Shelby looked like all his Christmases had come at once. "This could be the start of a great partnership."

"Well, we're not known as the spirit detectives for nothing." I laughed.

"Who's we?"

"Well, there's me and Frank. Elsie and Dorothy, Ana, and of course, Charlie."

"Where is Charlie?" Shelby asked.

That was a very good question, and I too was interested in the answer. Last night, after I'd defeated Amethyst, I'd drifted in and out of consciousness. The doctors had since explained to me that my body hadn't coped with all the exertion so soon after waking from a coma. However, a good night's sleep and some amazing drugs had me feeling a lot brighter, but I'd yet to see Charlie.

"I wanted to say thanks," Shelby continued. "Because of him I managed to crack the case." He beamed.

"He's getting a few things organized," Dorothy explained.

"You know, Daisy, when I entered that building behind Charlie last night and saw you levitating, I didn't know what to think." Shelby's forehead wrinkled as he squinted toward me and rubbed the back of his neck.

"Yeah, that was quite some initiation you had," I mused, feeling sympathy for him.

"So, are you—ummm—some kind of witch?" he asked, chewing the inside of his cheek.

"I am, or rather was, a night demon. It seems I had the power to use dreams to influence people. I could travel across space and time in my dreams and help people via theirs. What happened last night wasn't something I ever thought I could do. Nor will I ever do it again."

"Do you really think you've stripped Amethyst of her power?" Shelby asked.

"Yes. I tried to infiltrate someone's dreams last night, and I couldn't do it." I looked down at my hands unable to return Dorothy's gaze as she would know it was Charlie's mind I'd wanted to visit.

Other than the brief moment after breaking the spell, Charlie had been absent in my life since I'd woken from my coma, and I was beginning to worry. I'd wanted to know if he dreamt of me.

"Things got pretty hectic once we got there." Shelby slipped his cap through his fingers, recent memories dancing in his eyes.

"Thank goodness you arrived when you did. I had nothing left in me to fend off Amethyst after that. And I'm sure despite the fact she had no power, she still wanted to hit me over the head with her mortar." I grinned, ignoring the weight sitting in my belly.

"Yeah, if only looks were illegal."

"What happened to Lilli?" I asked. "Once the paramedics arrived, I don't recall seeing her."

"Another disappearance I'm afraid. She must have slipped out when my attention was elsewhere. Charlie followed her with someone I couldn't see named Ana, but the night consumed her. Don't worry, she'll have to resurface sometime, and when she does, we'll have her back in custody. The same goes for Amethyst. They can't stay hidden forever."

An ache started around my heart when I thought how much life had changed in such a short space of time. I'd lost too many friends, too many loved ones.

Dorothy placed her hand over mine, her heat radiating strength. I took it and squeezed, grateful for everything I had gained.

I parted my lips, wanting to tell her how much she had come to mean to me, when the door reopened, and the man who made me whole entered the room, a large bunch of yellow gerberas in his hands.

"Sorry it's taken me so long to get here," he said, his steps large and purposeful as he crossed the room closing the gap between us. "But you have no idea how far I had to go to get these." His smile revealed his crooked front teeth, the crinkles around his eyes deepening as he passed the flowers to me. "And I wanted them to be the first thing you saw when I arrived."

My heart stuttered, and my thoughts scattered as I fixated on the petals. Butterflies danced in my stomach as I accepted the bouquet, inhaling their happiness.

"Thank you," I wheezed, my breath suddenly stuck in my chest as all moisture on my lips dried.

"They're your favorite, right?" he asked, his movements momentarily halting.

I nodded as words escaped me, and he relaxed.

For the first time since I had met him, I could physically feel his presence. I could smell his minty breath and the aroma of his woody aftershave, his heat travelling the space between us. As he touched my hand, my entire body tingled, and I ached for him to move closer.

His smile was small and intimate as his finger lightly pushed a curl back from my forehead, before tracing a path toward my lips.

"It's so nice to finally meet the whole you, Daisy," he whispered.

The room disappeared as my world narrowed to only him. Blood pounded in my ears, and my body twitched as I became hyper-aware of his touch, and I yearned for him, the air between us palpable.

Charlie's eyes moved to my mouth as he cupped my chin. Placing a delicate kiss on my lips, he stole my breath as our souls connected. I sighed and reached for him, never wanting the moment to end.

"I've waited a long time for that," Charlie whispered close to my ear. "But it was worth every moment."

closed my eyes and took a deep breath before inserting the key into the lock. Crazy Daisy's, my little flower store I loved with all my heart, had been closed for a while, as my friend and employee, Monica, hadn't been able to keep the store running. But none of that mattered as the little bell above the door jingled and I crossed the threshold and entered my store for the first time since my attack.

The fresh flowers were missing, and the Christmas decorations were still hanging, but as the lingering scent of the season filled my lungs, I drew strength from its familiarity, allowing it to comfort me.

Spending the morning with my mom and sister had been draining. Our relationship needed a lot of work to make it right, but it seemed that my near-death experience had given them a new perspective. I was excited yet cautious to see where it would lead and relished the chance to spend more time with my grandpa. I missed him more than any of them and yearned to be close to him again.

My gaze roamed the room as I placed my mug of steaming hot coffee and bag on the counter and pulled my jacket tight. I then went in search of the thermostat, needing to warm the place up before I turned the sign on the door to *Open.* My first flower delivery would be here shortly, and I wanted everything to be perfect for the start of new day.

I moved through the small store taking stock of what was there. The wall behind the counter still held rows of brightly colored ribbon, hanging messy and loose. I straightened them before moving on to the flower wrap, lining the sheets up, ready to be used. The metal baskets were stacked, neatly waiting to be filled with the gerberas and white hydrangeas I'd ordered. White spider mums would mix with wax flowers and variegated pittosporum, and a flip in my belly betrayed just how excited I was to create some new bouquets. I just prayed I would get the orders for them and that my store would flourish once again.

Winter in Dandelion Ponds was always wet, the light sapping even the brightest of color from everything. But flowers changed that. They made even the dullest of days brighter. As the bell jingled once more, I straightened the timber hallstand, noting I needed to dust the small stock of decorator pots and glass vases.

I spun on my heel, expecting Leo, my delivery man. Instead, I froze as Lilli Alexander stood on the threshold.

Her head hung low; her eyes were guarded as she silently stepped inside. She looked tired, her cheeks hollowed, her mouth downturned.

She lifted her hand, palm facing me. "Before you tell me to leave, can you please listen to what I have to say?"

I straightened my shoulders, my back rigid. "Why should I?"

She swallowed hard. "Because I need to apologize. Then I'll disappear and never bother you again."

"You need to go to jail," I said, wishing my phone was in my jeans pocket and not in my bag so I could call the police.

"No. My mother will know where to find me if I go there."

"Why did you come back to Dandelion Ponds?"

"I didn't want to, but after my arrest I spent some time in jail waiting for my bail hearing. It gave me the chance to take a closer look at my actions, and I didn't like what I saw. Then one day I met a woman who claimed she knew my mother. They'd been friends when they were children, so she befriended me and kept me safe."

I scoffed. "As if you needed any help."

"You have no idea."

"You've been missing for some time. Why come back now?"

"There was something here that I needed. Daisy, are you aware of just how many covens are in this state?"

I took a beat to consider her words, before slowly shaking my head.

"I thought the night demons were the only ones." I shrugged.

Lilli gave me a pitiful look and sighed. "You're too naïve for your own good."

"Well, how many are there?" I demanded.

"I have no idea of the exact number, but it runs into the hundreds. And they're not all as nice as the night demons."

I gulped. "Lilli, why are you telling me this?"

"Because Mom's old friend told me things I never knew. Things about Dandelion Ponds and the secrets held here. I needed to come home and find them."

I shook my head and moved toward my bag, ready to call Shelby. "I know what you're doing," I cursed. "You're trying to suck me into your story, so I'll feel sorry for you. Well, it's not going to work this time."

"No, that's not it." Lilli rushed toward me and placed her hand over mine, preventing me from retrieving my phone. "Daisy, I don't have a lot of time, so you have to listen to me. I need to tell you something before I go."

I snatched my hand from her grasp and crossed my arms over my chest, my eyes narrowed at her.

"Well, I have questions for you too," I demanded.

"Fine. Ask away. What do you want to know?"

My mind jumbled as memories of our friendship flashed. Thoughts of what she did to me mixed with what she did to my friends, my family, but most of all Logan.

"Why did you loan Logan the money to buy that building but stopped me from doing so?"

"I didn't want you to have control of it. In fact, I tried hard to prevent you from even knowing about the building. I knew it wouldn't take you long to figure out what that site used to be."

"You have way too much faith in me."

She shook her head, her auburn locks swishing on her shoulder. "I never wanted my mother to know about the site either. By Logan owning it, I thought we could bury what it once was, and in his name my mother should never have been suspicious of it." Lilli scoffed. "I should have known better. Amethyst sticks her nose into everything I do, supervising everything for her own benefit."

"Did you show me the dream of how it all began?"

"What are you talking about?"

I hurriedly recalled the dream that had started it all. The more I spoke, the more confused Lilli looked.

"I have no idea what you're talking about." She mimicked my stance, as her brow knitted together.

"If it wasn't you, then who was it?" I asked, my own brow matching hers.

"You know you are a direct descendant of Valeria, right?"

I nodded.

"Then maybe Valeria planted the dream herself."

Goosebumps raced down my spine as I considered her words. "You think she wanted me to have the power of the garden?"

"I honestly have no idea, but maybe she wanted the garden to be brought back to life. You are the florist with a love for plants. You have more skills than anyone I know."

"But I never would have used the plants for evil."

"Then like everyone else, she underestimated you."

We both stood silent, lost in thought.

"If I could go back in time and change it all, Daisy, I would." Lilli moved to lean against the counter, her shoulders hunched, looking frailer than I had ever seen her. Her head hung low, as a single tear dripped off her chin. "I never thought she'd hurt Logan. Sure, she threatened me with it a lot, which is one of the reasons I agreed to marry Mark. If she thought Logan wasn't so important to me, she might have just left him alone. Like everything else, I was wrong." Her voice cracked as she swiped at the tear.

"You couldn't have stopped her, Lilli. She was far too powerful."

"You stopped her. You stopped us all."

I lifted a shoulder. "I had a lot of help, a lot of friends who gave me their strength."

Lilli nodded. "You've given me the inspiration to stand strong, to not let her rule me anymore. It'll never make amends for what I've done, but it may stop the evil my mother can cause."

"She can't hurt you anymore," I replied, wondering why I felt the need to comfort her. "The Lethal Garden died once the eclipse had passed."

"I've learned things, Daisy. Found things. Things that can harm a lot of people. I need to keep that information out of my mother's hands. I need to disappear."

"I should be thanking you for helping me that night, but I can't forgive you for what you've done." My limbs felt heavy as I sat on the nearest chair. "If it had just been me you hurt, then maybe. But you destroyed the lives of so many people I loved. Including your own."

"I never had a life." She sneered. "I was always under the control of my mother. Everything I did was to please her."

"Look where that got you."

"Which is why I need to go where she can never find me—not

so I can finally have a life of my own, but to stop her using the knowledge I have."

"Is it really that dangerous?"

"In the wrong hands, it has the potential to change the world. And not for the better."

"But now that the night demons have no power, what can Amethyst do?"

"Daisy, if she learns what I've learned, then life as we know it will cease." Lilli pushed off the counter and took a step toward the door. She stopped with her hand on the latch. "The knowledge needs to be buried somewhere far from here. Somewhere she will never find it."

"Wait! That's even more reason you need to tell me about it."

"I'm sorry. This is for the best. Everyone is safer if I just disappear. I'm sorry, Daisy. For everything. I wished I'd had this strength a long time ago. For what it's worth I really did enjoy our friendship."

She pulled the door open, and a blast of cold air rushed into the store before she stepped into the snow, her footsteps the only sign she was ever here.

I'm offering a free e-book to everyone who signs up to my mailing list.

www.bethprentice.com

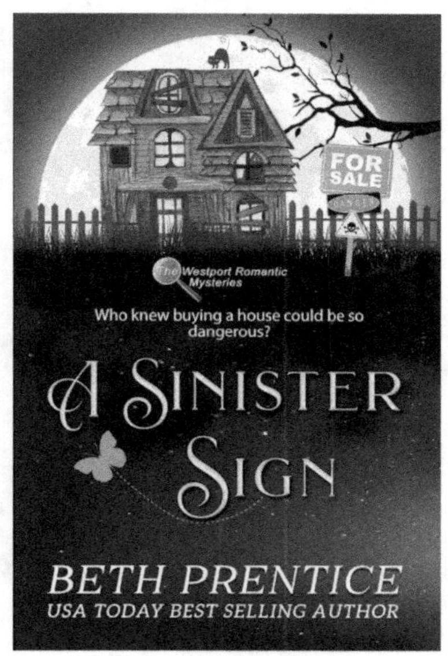

Who knew buying a house could be so dangerous?

Fed up with city life, Lizzie Fuller decides that moving home to the suburbs is just what she needs. But despite loving her family, the idea of living with them isn't all that appealing. And it doesn't take long to find the house of her dreams…or nightmares —it's really just a question of perspective.

The lonely run-down old Victorian in need of major renovations tugs on her heartstrings, and before she can stop herself, she's fallen head over heels in love with it. Unfortunately, she's not the only one who wants it, and the other bidders aren't playing nice.

Deadly accidents, missing real estate agents and a chilling stranger, are all sinister signs that this is not the house for her.

Still, Lizzie is determined to rescue this fixer upper or die trying. Now all she needs to do is to win the auction and stay alive.

If only it was that easy...

A Sinister Sign is the prequel to Lizzie's adventures in Westport. If you like crazy families, cozy reads, and a sweet romance, all tied together with a ribbon of danger, then you'll love The Westport Mysteries.

www.bethprentice.com

ABOUT THE AUTHOR

I'm Beth and I write funny, romantic mysteries (aka cozy mysteries), paranormal cozy mysteries, and the odd rom com because two of my favorite things are romance and mystery.

I'm the proud but often flustered owner of two dogs, two very noisy Indian Ringnecks, a Parrotlet named Axel, five chickens, and a duck named Dorothy. Oh, and I can't forget the Guinea Pig Herbie. I spend most of my days wishing for a quiet life but secretly loving the chaos!

When I'm not writing you can find me lost in a good book, passively watching documentaries (my hubby loves them and seems to have gained full control of the remote) and scrolling Instagram dreaming of holidays I don't have time to take, and perfect hair.

https://bethprenticebooks.com

www.ingramcontent.com/pod-product-compliance
Lightning Source LLC
Chambersburg PA
CBHW070952180726
48291CB00004B/1253